MISPLACED MISTLETOE

A HOLIDAY NOVELLA

ISABEL JOLIE

❀ Created with Vellum

No matter how many centuries back you go, no matter which religion or philosophy you choose, the reason for the season is love.

Eight Years Ago

NORA

"HI." HIS DARK, LONGISH HAIR FELL OVER HIS BROW, and he flicked it back, only for it to fall right back down again. He held a beer in his hand, and he stood close enough I got a whiff of the lemony hops. His steady gaze locked on me as if he mistook my red hair for peppermint, and he wanted a taste.

"Hi." My hand trembled as I held it out for a cordial handshake, but he didn't seem to notice. He lifted it and pressed his lips over my knuckles, suave and cool. A giggle escaped, and the room swayed, a sure sign those berry red holiday martinis packed more than sugar.

"I haven't seen you before." His deep, masculine drawl lured me in.

"Oh, I'm new." *And you don't sound like a New Yorker.*

"You look new." My skin tingled in the wake of his gaze, up and down my body. Heat circled me… maybe the packed room, maybe the alcohol, or maybe this cute, yummy guy leaning oh, so close.

"I mean, I've only been at Evolve for a week."

"They hired you right before the holidays? How'd you swing that?"

"Lucky, I guess."

"Lucky, what's your name?"

"Nora."

He repeated my name back to me slowly. His teasing smile, combined with the way he leaned into me, smacked of an abundance of confidence. If it weren't for the alcohol coursing through my veins, I might have heeded the warning.

"And what's your name?"

"Ashton." I liked the name, and I especially liked how it rolled off his tongue.

The closer he leaned, the more the faint scent of lemony hops grew, and I wondered how far down the V-neck of my velvet dress he could see.

"How long have you been at Evolve?" My

question sounded raspy, and I sucked back more of the sugary red liquid.

"I don't work at Evolve."

"Oh?" I'd assumed everyone gathered in my boss's tiny apartment worked together.

Hand-cut letters taped to the wall over the futon spelled out First Annual Chrismukkah Party. On the coffee table in the den sat a two-foot Christmas tree and a silver menorah. The tree had no lights, and the menorah had no candles, but the cooler on the floor in the kitchen was full of beer, and sticky red liquid dotted the narrow kitchen counter.

"I'm a doctor at St. Vincent's." Pride wrapped around his words, and as he pressed his arm against the refrigerator, effectively trapping me below him, I reveled in his hungry gaze. I liked this handsome man looking at me like I was the candy of the hour. *And Christmas surprise, he's not a colleague.*

"What kind of doctor?"

"The general kind." He removed his arm from over my head and shoved his hand in his pocket. "I'm a resident. In medical school. I'm applying for cardiology programs."

"Oh. Does that mean you'll be moving?"

"Maybe." *Bummer.*

"Where all have you applied?"

"A few hospitals here. Iowa. Seattle. California."

"I'm from Iowa."

"Oh, you are? That explains it."

"Explains what?"

"Your wholesome glow. You look out of place here. You're not wearing black."

The metal protrusion on the back of my candy cane earring pressed into the pad of my thumb as I played with it. With his comment, my love for my five-dollar Goodwill find, a Banana Republic green velvet dress, incinerated. I'd wanted something that said holiday and wore a necklace with blinking red and green lights that I purchased for ten cents next to the cash register. But as I looked around the room, black dominated the scene. That and sequin tiny tops paired with jeans or butt-hugging pants. All the other women exhibited sexy and cool. New York chic. I reeked of Iowa.

"Hey, I like it." He slung his arm back over my head and whispered next to my ear, "I like it a lot." His warm breath brushed my skin and tingles scurried all over me.

"Where are you from?" *Don't tell me New York. I won't buy it.* He dressed like all the other men, but that drawl….

"Born in Savannah." I smiled. I'd never been there before, but I'd read enough books that featured the southern city, I felt like I had. "Georgia," he added with emphasis.

"Nice." I waffled on my feet. The soundtrack

shuffled into another holiday song. I closed my eyes, singing along with Stevie Wonder to the lyrics of *Someday at Christmas*.

"You like this song?" he asked.

I leaned against the yellow refrigerator, inches from the good-looking man as Stevie sang about one day men not being boys. The young doctor smelled like cedar, and I'd willingly bet my last wrinkled dollar bill was all man. Up until that moment, the total of my experience had been boys. I hoped that here in the big bad city, I'd get to experience men.

We huddled out of the way of others in the back of the narrow galley kitchen. Out of the corner of my eye, a copywriter from the office bent over the cooler.

"Nora." Ashton sang my name, pronouncing the *ora* long and slow, drawing my inebriated attention back to him.

"Yeah?" I teasingly drew out the vowels.

He pointed his index finger skyward. His chocolate eyes danced, and a boyish smirk flicked across his lips. He'd pulled me over here to talk on purpose. Positioned me below the mistletoe hanging in front of a refrigerator with an objective in mind.

"You owe me a kiss. Christmas spirit and all."

It sounded like he said, "ya'll." I giggled…because red martinis. His hand curved around my hip bone, effectively halting the giggles.

"I've never kissed an Iowan." I blinked. Swallowed.

"I've never kissed a Savannah-han."

"You butchered that word." The smirk returned.

Then he lowered his lips to mine. The room faded to black. I clutched his bicep for balance, the muscle firm and hard beneath my fingers. His nose brushed mine, and a burst of white lights twinkled beneath my closed eyelids. If I were a Christmas tree, then that gentle brush of his lips served as the timer clicking on because everything inside me lit up. The Rockefeller Christmas tree personified. Or maybe he was the tree because I kind of wanted to climb him.

"Excuse me. I'm sorry. I need to get in the fridge." Mortified, I pushed away.

"Don't worry about it, doll. Just need to get my vodka." The tall woman opened the freezer while I backed up against the counter. Ashton leaned against the opposite counter, and I felt his gaze on me everywhere.

One or two curious looky-loos cast glances our way. The last thing I wanted, as the new hire, was to build a reputation as the girl who hooked up at parties. Hooking up with a stranger in my new boss's apartment had to fall in the things-you-just-don't-do list. But I very much wanted to keep talking to this extremely attractive man with a sexy smile who also happened to be a really good kisser. In an uncharacteristically forward moment, I pushed onward. I'd wanted to make it in the big bad city for as long as I could remember. *This is my time.*

"Do you want to maybe get out of here? Go someplace else?"

HAPPY CHRISTMAS (WAR IS OVER)

resent Day - Eight Years Later

NORA

THE ELEVATOR DOORS OPEN, AND AN UPBEAT *JINGLE Bells* melody replaces the barely audible elevator Mannheim Steamroller symphony. One week to go until all holiday music disappears, not to be heard again for another nine or so months. Not that I'm counting.

Delilah, my longtime colleague and friend, wiggles three fingers in the air, and Justin, our agency's receptionist, clasps both palms together in a prayer motif. Three hours to go. They are counting down.

The Evolve ad agency closes for a week at five o'clock. Half the office has already cleared out. At one second past five, the lights behind the reception desk will go dark, not to be flipped on until the new year.

"Catch, Nora!" Delilah calls out as a peppermint candy whizzes past my head and crashes against the wall. "Gotta be faster. Here's another."

"Stop." I hold up my palm as this woman needs visual cues. "No, thank you." A waft of starchy scent burns my nostrils and itches my throat. "Why does it smell like a Christmas tree in your office?" The only tree in her office is a three-foot fake one sitting on a side table beside the loveseat.

"I've been testing spritzers. Do you like this?" She points a canister in my direction, and a white cloud singes my eyeballs. "Smell."

"No." *Gross.*

"You don't like the smell of Christmas trees? Aw, sugar. Everyone likes the smell of a good fir. Are you just saying that because you're still mad you broke your ankle carrying that tree up the stairs two years ago?"

"No. That scent is too artificial."

With a loud clang, the canister hits the inside of her metal trash can.

"I know." She sounds resigned. "A lot of the scents are too harsh, don't you think? We need subtle. Non-drying."

I plop down in her guest chair and kick my feet up on the coffee table. I spent yesterday organizing my email inbox. There is nothing for me to do.

"Do you have any last-minute shopping? Any last-minute errands?"

"Nope." I gnaw at the plastic wrapping on a peppermint stick, attempting to tear it open, until Delilah's silence unnerves me.

"What?"

"You really just don't like Christmas, do you?"

"I like it fine." And I do. It's fine. It's not my favorite holiday. But it's fine. No family means I spend the day holed up in my apartment. Sometimes I go out to a movie theater and watch with all the other non-Christians in the city. But even they are usually with family. It's not like I don't receive invitations to join others' family celebrations…but I decided long ago that I don't like being the odd man out. The one-of-these-things-is-not-like-the-others theme song running through my head never mollifies me, ever. It's not that I hate Christmas. I'm not the Grinch. But I don't love the holiday. There are people who live for Christmas, and I am not one of them.

Delilah's head twists to the side, and her lips

pucker, and I suspect she's a nanosecond from hopping out of her desk chair and hugging me.

"All right." With an official clap of my hands, I ask, "So what remains to be done for tonight?"

Delilah smiles, one of her big, jubilant smiles. She bounces a bit in her seat. Those blue eyes literally twinkle in that way she has when she's up to something I'm not going to like. *Oh...shit.*

"I have a list of all the single men," Delilah announces. *And there it is.*

"You do know you're married, right?"

She waves at me like I'm being silly. I asked to be funny, but I know damn well what she is up to. The woman before me has set me up on some of the worst blind dates of my life. Delilah and I have worked together for eight years, and she's been married for close to five of them. That's left her with far too much time to think about my single status.

"Of course I know that. But you aren't. And neither is Amelia from accounting."

"And what, exactly, do you have in mind?" A dull pain throbs, and I rub my left temple. She's leaving tomorrow to go home for the week. Anything she is concocting can be ignored until forgotten.

Delilah lifts a large brown cardboard box from somewhere behind her desk.

"I volunteered to hang the mistletoe. You wanna join me? We can take a cab to Chelsea and be back here super-fast." She sets the box down on her desk and does her jazz hands thing, waving her hands and fingers. "Ta daaa."

I fail to see how mistletoe relates to the singles list, but I leave it alone, hoping her brain has traveled beyond the topic.

"I thought they hired a fancy-schmancy event planning company?" I ask.

"Oh, Olivia did. But she's letting me do this. I love hanging the mistletoe. I've been in charge of the mistletoe since the very first Christmakkah party. Remember that one? In Anna and Olivia's apartment on 82nd Street?" *I could never forget it.*

"We've come a long way, huh?" she asks, and I nod in agreement. But, really, it's Olivia, Anna, and Delilah who have come a long way. It's not just that they're all married, and Olivia and Delilah have kids, but Olivia and Anna married men who are loaded and now foot the bill for an insanely expensive holiday party each year. As for me, my life is more or less the same. I no longer have a roommate, which is huge in this city, but other than my own pad and a raise in title and salary, I'm pretty much the same.

Knock, knock, knock.

Anna, our boss and friend, crosses the threshold. She's wearing her signature jeans and Chucks, but her hair has been professionally blown out in preparation for tonight. The glamorous waves contrast with her casual Friday ensemble. "What's that?"

"Mistletoe." Delilah beams, looking so damn proud. I suck on my peppermint stick and strive to ignore her. She doesn't mean to be annoying; she just is.

"All right." Anna crosses her arms in front of her chest and faces me, essentially dismissing the jubilant blonde. "Nora, I've emailed your number out to the executive staff and all account managers. I cc'd you. You have my cell. I hate we do this to you every year. Next year, we really need to find someone else to be on call." Her emphasis on *really* is super sweet, but we both know it'll be me again next year.

"It's no biggie. Besides, nothing ever comes up." When the agency closes for the week between Christmas and New Year's, they ask that one senior-level art director remain available should any client emergencies arise. The kinds of emergencies they envision are quick fixes, such as an advertisement correction, but a call tree exists should anything come up a sole art director couldn't handle. If any of our clients had a true emergency, we'd pull a team together, and we'd be there for them.

"So, Anna, what do you think of Nora and Ben from the Heineken account?" I shoot a heated glare Delilah's way. Not that there is anything wrong with

Ben, but he isn't my type. And we work together. And I don't want to be set up.

Delilah wiggles a printout. "No worries. Singles list." When she smiles, my insides churn with annoyance.

Anna turns to me in confusion, and I simply shake my head. There's nothing to say. Delilah wishes I had a significant other. I get it. I'm the last single girl standing. It's awkward to have a seventh wheel.

Sam had a friend, Jason, who had been a fun grump to hang out with at times, but he went off and not only got married but moved to Chicago. He and his wife Maggie never make it out for this party, instead choosing to meet up with everyone in Aspen.

For several years, Chase, one of our friends, was also single, and that worked out well. He and I hung out without issue. Then he went off and got married. So, not just the last single woman standing...I'm the last person standing. Hence blondie and her mission.

Anna glances between Delilah and me and decides she is not getting into it. "I've got to run. I need to have everything packed before the party tonight. Jackson wants to hit the road first thing in the morning."

"How is that smart?" Delilah asks, looking at Anna like she just announced she's sacrificing an unborn child. "I insisted we book a later afternoon flight. No one wants to be mobile after drinking heavily the night before. If I had my way, we wouldn't leave until Sunday, but my mom had a hissy fit, so…"

"How did you end up splitting the time with Mason's mom? Are you flying back on Christmas?" Anna asks her.

"No. She's flying down and spending it with us. Staying through the New Year. I don't like traveling on Christmas. You're lucky you don't have to worry about that. You can just stay with Jackson's family." Delilah slaps her hand over her mouth in her over-the-top way as she simultaneously swallows her foot, so to speak. "Oh, I didn't mean that, sweetie. I mean, obviously, you'd rather your parents be here."

The need to get out of the office before either one of them remembers my situation and casts pitying expressions in my direction hits me hard.

I am one step into the hall when Delilah asks, "What about Ashton? Is he going down to Virginia this year?"

I don't dare raise my eyes or turn around, but my retreat halts.

"No. He's refusing to. He says he'd rather not spend his Christmas with Jackson's family. He says he'll enjoy it and that he can use the break. He works such long hours. And I guess selfishly. I need him to dog sit."

I'd spent more than one Christmas with other people's families, so I understood Ashton's perspective.

Delilah half chuckles, half snorts. "Do you remember that time you asked me to dog sit?"

I quietly escape down the hall. I've heard that story a thousand times.

THE CAB STOPS ON THE CORNER OF HUDSON AND Greenwich. One glance at my watch confirms my prompt arrival for the last holiday party of the season. This one last holiday commitment is all that stands between me and my sofa, wine, and the Hallmark Channel.

Make an appearance, float between friends, have your two allotted drinks, then return home to begin one glorious week of solitude.

After handing over a fat holiday tip—because, hey, it's Christmastime—I exit the cab and pull my black coat tight around me. My red stilettos scratch the sidewalk as I fall in line behind several other well-dressed couples making their way to the Tribeca Rooftop.

Warm, dry air blasts over me, ruffling my hair. As I pass my coat over to coat check, I catch a glimpse of myself in the enormous wall mirror. The green dress sandwiched between pale white legs, red hair, and stilettos is beyond Christmassy. I suck in my stomach and push my shoulders back, but better posture does nothing to mitigate the effect. I wish I'd realized my LBD had faded. Because I yearn to be wearing black. No, scratch that. I yearn to be home, on my sofa, underneath a blanket, comfy and warm.

"Nora?" A friend from the account management team approaches. Of course, she has a date, so after introducing us, I join the two of them in the elevator.

"I've always wanted to check this place out." It's not clear if she's speaking to me or her date, but we have several floors to climb, so I share.

"Delilah recommended it. She's stoked. The party planner did a phenomenal job. It's gorgeous." I managed to duck out on hanging mistletoe, but she'd texted photos.

"How many did they invite?"

"I heard two hundred and fifty?" It wasn't my party to plan, but I heard a lot of the details.

"Have you met Sam before? He's the one who throws the party, right?" If by *throws*, she means pays for, then the answer is yes. But I remember the humble beginnings of this holiday celebration among friends. It was better then.

My colleague's date asks, "Do you think we'll

meet Sam Duke?" I smile. Everyone wants to cut a deal with the billionaire.

"If you keep an eye out for him, you'll see him. He's a nice guy." I add the last bit to remind these two that Sam is, above all else, a human being. I can't call him my BFF, but I do know his wife Olivia well. He was one of those in the "right place at the right time" stories. He saw a need for website e-commerce, built a great platform, and the rest, as they say, is history. But he wasn't one of those people who let his money go to his head.

Anna, my boss, and Olivia have been best friends since college. Olivia met Sam when she took an internship at his office. And that's how I, a little nothing from Iowa, became friends with a billionaire.

The elevator doors ding open, and we all peer out, spellbound. The photos Delilah texted did not do the venue justice. Brilliant, twinkling white Christmas lights crisscross the ceiling, and a plethora of trees, dusted in faux snow, line the perimeter of the entry and through the open doorways into a winter fantasyland. Exposed brick lines the walls, and two sides of the open room boast floor-to-ceiling windows and black iron grids. High above, a massive skylight exposes hundreds of small lit stars hung across the space, creating a semblance of magical sky. Chances are none of those are real stars, as here in the city, a sparkling night sky eludes us, but the effect of the electrical lights high above is so enchanting it's better than the real thing.

"There you are!" Delilah squeals. Her husband Mason follows closely behind. He's in a black tux, and she's wearing a red sequined dress. Her blonde hair hangs down her back in long, bouncy waves. "Is this place not insane? Olivia way outdid herself this time."

"It's stunning." I give her a hug. Then Mason bends to hug me too.

"My parents have been throwing holiday parties for years, and I've never seen anything like this. You've got to come out on the roof deck. They've got a maze of trees, a craft cocktail bar, a wine bar, and a snow machine! We can't stay out there, though…that stuff can't be good for the hair. But you've gotta see it."

"Your parents throw a lot of parties?" I ask.

Mason's eyebrows lift, and he mouths, "Oh, yes."

"In New Orleans. My dad's a business owner. It's one of those things. Something that's expected. I'm sure that's part of the reason Sam now floats the bill for this party. It's a business expense for him. At a certain point, you can't be throwing parties and not invite your most valued clients."

That's a world I have no desire to understand. I

am perfectly content living my life as an employee. She grabs my hand and tugs.

"Have you seen any cuties yet?" she asks into my ear.

"I just got here." I emphasize *just* and roll my eyes at Mason. He smirks. Delilah's heart is in the right place, but she's completely forgotten what it's like to be single. If she remembered, she'd know that holiday parties like this are mostly attended with dates. I did scan my Tinder picks, searching for a date contender. And I'd come close to inviting someone…that is, if you consider a finger hovering over the phone close.

"Hot chocolate? Hot toddies?" A woman dressed in a Santa's helper outfit holds out a tray with menus. She stands in front of a life-sized gingerbread house.

"Do you want? Or would you prefer wine?" I answer Delilah's question with wine, and Mason answers with beer. She leads the way.

A couple of years ago, a friend held her wedding in this space, but on this night, I barely recognize the space. I follow Delilah alongside Mason, taking in all the sights. A live band belts out holiday music covers, but it's the saxophone in the front that catches my attention. He's so good that guests stop dancing and stare.

I'm completely taken in by the band, but Delilah

misunderstands. "Is this not unreal? I swear, I think they spent easily two hundred grand. Anna said Jackson told her he'd seen an estimate that said three hundred and twenty dollars per head. But I'd bet they paid easily twice what the food cost on decoration expense."

"Wow." It's the response Delilah expects. As we stand in line, in what I hope is a line for alcohol, I check out all the long, stunning gowns.

"I'm feeling a bit too cocktail," I admit. My fingers brush my velvet dress, an above-the-knee number. It isn't the dress I planned on wearing, but after finding a stain on my reliable little black dress, I found this one with a tag on it crammed in the back of my closet.

"The invite said to dress for a wonderland. That means anything goes. You look adorable." *Fantastic. That's what I was going for.*

"De-li-lah!" We all turn to face the screeching sound. Delilah drops my hand to bear hug a woman I've never seen before.

Mason steps forward and embraces her. I back away and scout the perimeter for a wine bar because we haven't been in line for the bar. Through the arched doorway, I see we've been in line for the roof deck. *No, thanks, give me the bar.*

I spy another life-sized gingerbread house designed to look like a ski chalet. Wine racks hang all along one side in lieu of skis. A bartender stands behind the bar, which doubles as the front of the themed hut. I make eye contact with the Santa hat-wearing bartender, and a suited man steps in front of me. His back removes the bartender from view. He slings his arm over a woman in a full-length sparkly white column dress. *Fantastic.*

"There you are!" Delilah calls from behind me. Mason offers a sympathetic smile. Delilah loops her arm through mine and leads me out of the high-ceilinged room.

"I couldn't hang mistletoe anywhere in here. They wouldn't let me up on the ladder. Something about insurance. But all down these halls, and toward the bathrooms…" Her smile spreads wide, and red lip gloss stains one front tooth. "If you see a yummy single guy, remember, these are the areas you should lead him."

My annoyance crests. I stop short. "There aren't any single guys here."

"Nope. Remember? I made a list. Checked it twice."

"Were you checking to see if they were naughty or nice?" I backtrack, returning to the bar. She follows.

"No, silly. I checked marital status on LinkedIn. Also eliminated anyone who listed 'in a relationship.'"

She opens her slim handbag. There's an actual list of names.

"And there's someone I want you to meet."

"De-li-lah," I whine. It's not that I'm against meeting men. I'm not. Really. But I can't stand the fluttery sensations in my stomach before a date. And I don't trust Delilah one bit. The girl can be embarrassing. She's one of those friends who will place me in front of an unsuspecting guy and say something like, "You're both single, and it's been ages since she's gotten any. You should both talk." That's never fun. For anyone.

"There he is. Come on."

I dig my five-inch heels into the hard polished concrete floor, refusing to budge. "He's probably here on a date. You know, not married doesn't mean single."

The strap on my red stiletto cuts into my foot on the side, and the temperature in the room rises as more party revelers pour off the elevator. The line at the bar is now four deep.

"Oh, sugar. Come on. I'm not trying to set you up. I just want you to meet someone."

Mason laughs out loud.

"Can we just get a glass of wine?" *Is that too much to ask?*

"I'll go get you both something. What do you want?"

I love Mason. "Thank you."

Delilah strides out of sight, presumably to chase down the man she wants to mortify me in front of. I move to follow Mason to the bar, but then I spot Anna beside a Christmas tree bedecked in mermaids. I'm taken in by the variety of mermaids in holiday themes. One of the paper-mâché mermaids holds a list and wears a blue Santa-shaped hat.

"Nora, I love that dress." Anna typically wears jeans and Converse sneakers in the office, but tonight she's gorgeous in a short black dress and heels.

"Have I introduced you to my brother?"

My insides seize as my gut crunches. I can't swallow. My gaze travels from Anna's black pointed heels to the men's shoes near her feet, then travels inch by inch, up the black suit slacks to the white shirt to the green tie with tiny red dots, to the lips I've tried to forget since my first Chrismukkah party eight years ago. A lifetime ago when these parties were held in an eight-hundred-square-foot apartment, and only friends attended, often in jeans, and there were no bartenders or a line to get a drink.

His chestnut hair is now trimmed and sways over his forehead, hanging just above those dark eyebrows and honey brown eyes. His clean-shaven jaw reminds me of a time when it wasn't smooth and resulted in raw sensitivity around my lips, throat, and thighs. The heat in the packed room reaches inferno level.

"Ashton." He extends a hand with a bored expression. *Shoot me now.* He has no idea who I am. I stare at his hand a beat too long. One dark eyebrow raises in question.

"Have you two ever met? I call him Bobby. But he insists on Ashton," Anna says, oblivious to my struggle to continue breathing and maintain cool.

"You're the only one who calls me Bobby." Ashton withdraws his offered hand and slips it into his trouser pocket. His attention is on his sister.

"Nice to meet you. I'm going to go get a drink." I rush the words and head off in the direction Mason went. *Wine. I need wine.*

I approach the gingerbread house wine bar with renewed determination. I have no idea where Mason went, but I need fortification. I catch Mr. Santa Hat's eye and hold up a finger. "Red, please."

He pushes a pre-filled glass my way as a deep, husky voice flows over my shoulder. Tingles cascade down my spine.

"I'll have red too, please," Ashton says.

I step forward, away from the bar, away from the man who doesn't recognize me. I refuse to turn around. I refuse to look him in his face. What is he doing here, anyway? He hasn't been at one of these parties in eight years. Long, skilled fingers lightly touch my shoulder.

"Nora?" With that one tentative word, he asks if I am angry. He asks if everything is okay. At least, that's how I interpret my name spoken with a lilt at the end. And I am not angry. The Ghost of Christmas Past doesn't haunt me.

Back then, I had zero expectations. I'd known he had other priorities. Alcohol. I blame alcohol for what happened between us. And with that thought, the red, red wine in my glass loses some appeal. I don't want to turn around. I don't want to face him.

"Nora?" Now he sounds curious. *Bloody Harry. I have no choice.*

"Hi." The single word comes out harsh. Flat. Possibly mean. It is not as intended.

"You may remember me as Bobby. I can't remember which name I introduced myself as back then." *You couldn't even remember me.* "Everyone knows me as Ashton. Now."

"Ashton," I repeat the word, dumbfounded. His name doesn't matter. I remember him. Robert Ashton Daughtridge.

"So, do you still work for my sister?"

"I do." I risk a glance upward into inquisitive brown eyes.

"She hasn't mentioned you in so long. I assumed you'd moved on." *Right.*

"No, I'm still at Evolve. Good to see you."

I step away without waiting to see if he has more to say.

In my peripheral vision, a black tuxedo crowds me. The tingles continue along my spine as I weave through the crowd. I push outside onto the rooftop, into cooler air. I open my mouth to suck it in. The crowd of revelers forces my steps to slow, matching the pace circulating through the forest of rooftop trees. Snowflakes whizz lightly through the air. Somewhere on the perimeter, snow machines toil.

"It's been a long time. How have you been?" he asks. *He's not going away. Face the music.*

I spy a path off to the side, free of people. *Ignoring him is rude.* And his sister has, in some ways, become my adopted family. *Get over yourself. Do this.*

"I've been good. How about you?"

"I've been good." He sips his wine, and I gaze longingly at the nearby exit. "I'm a doctor now. I mean, technically, I was before, when we…I'm a surgeon now." *Right.*

"Anna keeps us updated." He raises a single eyebrow. "From time to time, you come up in staff meetings. Not often." I don't want to make it sound like I've been keeping up with him for eight years. Even if I've listened intently to every single word Anna has ever shared about him, the last thing I want is for it to sound like that. "She never mentioned you changed your name."

"I didn't really… my name is Robert Ashton. My parents called me Bobby, but when I went off to college, I introduced myself as Ashton. And med school, obviously." He shrugs. "She still slips sometimes."

"Well, I guess most people call you Dr. Daughtridge, anyway."

"Most people do." He smirks. His broad shoulders seem even broader in his tux, and he's completely comfortable in his skin. As confident now as I remember. "So, how many years has it been? Let's see. I was a third-year, is that eight years?"

Knowing what event he is cavalierly counting back from churns my stomach. All those pre-date sensations I can't stand hit me tenfold. I liked it better when he didn't remember me at all.

"Eight years ago. Time flies, huh? So, what kind of surgeon?"

I gaze through the crowd, seeking someone else to talk to, and Ashton notices. I can tell by the way he tilts his head and inches closer like he did that night in front of the yellow refrigerator.

"Heart."

"You specialize in hearts?" My brain has frozen.

The correct word eludes me, and in place, I let out a double entendre. *I should just go home.*

He licks his lower lip, and he smirks. My stomach twists into a painful knot, and I place my palm over it.

"Cardiologist. That's right. When we met before, I didn't yet know my specialty or where I'd end up."

"You had applied all around."

"I ended up here. But you waxed poetic about Iowa." I focus on the crowd milling through the elaborate forested maze. "Your eyes are bluer than I remember. Maybe it's the eyeliner and dark shadow."

Is he really commenting on my makeup? Of course, I only recently learned how to apply eyeliner, so I suppose it is a new look for me.

"I'd thought for sure you'd return home. When Anna didn't mention you, I'd assumed you'd moved back." I ignore the lamest excuse I've ever heard. "Do you still live in the city?"

I lift my chin and face that confident brown smirk and answer, "No roommates." It feels like I'm waving a hard-earned trophy in his face.

"Same place?" His question rings with disbelief, and I bark out a laugh.

"No. Of course not. I now live in a one-bedroom. A true one bedroom." Only in New York did that definition mean something. "And I don't wait tables anymore."

"Nice. Glad to see my sister has been treating you well."

"Well, I'm glad I ran into you." I force a smile. "Congratulations on cardiology." Guilt nudges me as he squints like he's trying to figure me out, or he can't believe I'm ending this awkward conversation. To soften my goodbye, I add, "Your sister is very proud of you."

You can see the pride Anna feels in her big brother whenever she speaks about him. I give a quick nod and sidestep to his right. His palm lands on my bare upper arm. Goosebumps scatter. His touch short-circuits my barely functioning brain.

He raises his eyebrows and jerks his head, motioning upward.

"We're under the mistletoe." I glance up, and sure enough, one of the red and green balls hangs high above us.

Delilah did not say she hung that here.

He grins. Eight years ago, our first kiss happened under mistletoe.

"That's not supposed to be there." His expression is both quizzical and amused. He hovers above me, ready for a kiss. It's clear he doesn't get it. "Delilah's setting me up with someone tonight. I need to go find her." For added impact, I singsong, "Love, peace and ho, ho, ho."

I push forward, determined to not stop this time. My nonsensical goodbye probably won't mean a thing to him, but given those were the last words he said to me, well, I don't think it's ever felt so good to say "ho, ho, ho."

Eight Years Ago

NORA

"YOU DON'T LIVE FAR AWAY?" THE HEAT FROM HIS hand burned through my long, puffy winter coat. The icy wind whipped as we stepped onto the sidewalk, and he clutched his coat collar around his neck. My unattractive glob of a coat, donated by a nice church family, handled winter. His waist-length jacket would never cut it in January back home.

"No. Not far." The cold air sobered me up. *What am I doing? What will he think if I suggest we return to the party?* "But I have nothing to drink. I just moved in a week ago."

"We'll duck in a deli and pick up a bottle. I can't stay out late because of work tomorrow, but I'd like to hang out and get to know you." He guided me along the sidewalk. I followed him because I'd never been on that block, or this area of the city before, in my life. Yes, I lived nearby, but everything felt foreign. Four days in, and I was hands down a newbie at New York City.

"You're working on Sunday?"

"Residents work all the time. And I need to study too. I can't let a day go by without getting some work in. I'd say we could go back to my place, but I have two roommates. And they're probably studying."

"On a Saturday night?"

"We're all in med school."

"Right. That makes sense." Inside the deli, six different wine bottles lined one shelf beside the ramen noodles. Even under the harsh fluorescent light, Ashton looked good. Really good. His tousled dark hair needed a trim. It fell over his eyebrows, past his eyelashes, and he kept pushing it back. The result was astoundingly sexy but also model-level alluring. He paid for a bottle of red with a rumpled bill he pulled out of his worn leather wallet. The cashier placed the bottle in a brown paper bag. *I'm really gonna do this.*

"I hope I have a wine opener," I muttered after we exited the deli. Talk about things I should've thought about earlier. How embarrassing if we got up to my humble abode and had no way to open his purchase.

"Do you have roommates?" *Hadn't I told him that?*

"I do. I have three of them." After a couple of cold, wordless blocks, we arrived at my apartment building. The metal door leading into the tight vestibule had been heavily scratched. Someone had etched in the phrase, "Love Means Love." When I'd seen it the first time, I'd taken it as a good omen. What a great message to see each day.

I turned my key in the lock, and he pushed the heavy door open. A rank, stale smell filled the hallway. I led the way to the stairs. Scratched, worn metal protected the edge of each stair. Dirt filled the crisscross pattern.

"My roommates aren't home. They all left yesterday to go home for Christmas. Are you going home for Christmas?" I asked as we climbed.

"No. Well, I suppose you could say the city is my home. I'll get together with my sister when I'm not working. Christmas isn't our favorite holiday."

It wasn't my favorite either. I liked the decorations and the music, but the season always underscored the things I didn't have. I reached the top of the fifth floor, slightly winded.

When I first responded to the ad, it had thrilled me to find an apartment in Manhattan with rent I could afford. I thought it was the most awesome apartment on the planet. However, with a guest in tow, a swash of embarrassment flushed over me.

The single room had two bunk beds built on wood boards nailed together. Someone, before my time, had gone to a hardware store and purchased two by fours and nailed them together. Thin twin mattresses covered the plywood. In one corner, a door to a bathroom remained open, exposing the tiny toilet, sink, and minuscule corner shower with a mildewed shower curtain. Open shelving covered the wall below the window and across from the counter with a sink and a dorm-sized refrigerator. The open shelving served as our only closet, and it overflowed with sweaters, t-shirts, and jeans. Bras hung messily down from each pole. One futon sat in the middle of the floor, as there was no available wall space. It was here, in the middle of the chaos, we sat to share a bottle of wine in two plastic cups. Me with a blue cup, and him with a black cup with a skull on it.

"What's it like when all four of you are in here?" So, the place wasn't the greatest. But for eight hundred dollars a month, I could afford it—sort of. Rent consumed half of my monthly income.

"Well, it's only been a week. But last week, we weren't ever all home at the same time."

"Do they work nights?"

"One of my roommates has a boyfriend, and he stays at his place a lot. Another roommate does work nights. He's a janitor who, I guess, cleans corporate buildings? His dream is to be an actor, so he cleans at night to free up his days for auditions. And then my other roommate is a hairdresser. She works sporadic hours. She's been around at night. But yeah, I imagine with all four of us in here, well, we'll barely fit on the futon." I pulled my legs up under me, settling into my corner. I studied him, curious about his background. A part of me wondered if he might be like me. "What's your story?"

"What do you mean?" He gave me that sexy, playful grin. *Jeez, they don't make 'em like this back in Decorah.*

I hated it when people pushed me for information about my past, yet I couldn't help but wonder if this guy who didn't like Christmas might be like me. What were the chances? That in my first week in a ginormous city, I'd run into a fellow foster kid? The urge to discover his past won out, and I asked him the direct question, "Your parents. Why aren't they in the picture at Christmas?"

"My parents passed away."

"I'm sorry. I shouldn't have—"

"It's okay. My dad died last year. My mom years before that. I'm lucky. I had them around through high school." *That is lucky.*

"They must've been young?" I guessed he couldn't be much over twenty-five or twenty-six.

"Doesn't bode well for my future." He grinned, then the plastic cup covered his face as he chugged the wine.

"What do you mean?" I didn't understand.

"My genes."

"Oh." I should've gotten that. "Is that why you became a doctor?"

"Maybe. My dad wanted me to follow his path, but I didn't really take to engineering. I preferred science. My experience makes me a more empathetic doctor, I think. At least more empathetic to my patients' families. I know what they're going to go through if we don't, you know, heal a patient."

I leaned forward and placed my hand over his, on his thigh. At that moment, he claimed the first sliver of my heart.

resent Day

ASHTON

PEACE, LOVE, AND HO, HO, HO. THAT SOUNDS LIKE something I might've said back in the day. One of my fellow residents, Palin, used to say it all the time. I haven't heard anyone utter that phrase since med school.

Her auburn hair flashes brunette in the shadows, and the true reddish hues shine through when the lights hit right. I follow from a distance as she meanders through the party. This party is a compilation of individuals from different companies and my sister's friends through the years. No one here knows every single person, but she greets several in the crowd. She has probably invited a significant number of colleagues from her ad agency.

My little sister has a solid group of friends. And I couldn't ask for a better brother-in-law. But I spend the bulk of my time at the hospital, so I don't see this crew often. I've declined countless invitations to my sister's friends' parties over the years. At first, I didn't have a choice. Over the holidays, in hospitals, low men on the totem pole pull the shifts. Once, a few years ago, I'd been in a tux, ready to meet up with this crew, when I got called in for emergency surgery.

The deep green dress fits snugly against Nora's curves. She teeters on sky-high, ruby red fuck-me heels. Most of the men here have dates, but I catch more than one man cast a second glance her way. It's that finely shaped ass. With that additional five inches, the top of her head reaches my chin.

She's even more beautiful than I remembered. She's come into her own. When Anna first introduced us tonight, I'd been scanning the crowd, searching for a green-eyed girl I'd never quite forgotten. I'd been curious to see if she might be here. I could've asked Anna, but I didn't. I'd studiously avoided mentioning Nora over the last eight years.

And there she was, standing before me.

Eight years ago, she'd been so young. She looked more like a high school girl than a college graduate, more skin and bones than sexy curves. Back then, I'd found her plenty sexy, but those big green eyes teemed with innocence, excitement, and hope. Nora had been the kind of girl who deserved to be wined and dined. She deserved to find a man with the time to introduce her the right way to this concrete jungle. Someone who would stand back and let her shake it all out on the dance floor with her friends but step in if a drunk got the wrong idea. Someone who could take her to the Hamptons in the summer and Vermont in the winter and to the pubs and clubs.

My sister Anna led that life. As did Anna's friends. Sure, I escaped the grind every now and then. But being hungover at work isn't an option when someone's life hangs in the balance. Being short on sleep, being hungry, being dazed, none of those are acceptable for someone in my profession.

I can understand why she's being frosty with me. I owed her a phone call. I don't have a great excuse. I always meant to call, then too much time passed. But it's been eight years. Surely the statute of limitations is in effect.

Come to think of it, Anna's colleague, the one married to a veterinarian, texted me earlier. She wanted to inquire if I was currently dating someone. I might've been a little short with her, and she'd responded with a litany of emojis and texted that if I maintained a social profile, she wouldn't have to reach out. At the time, I'd found her intrusion into my day to be aggravating, but it's conceivable I'll need to ask my sister for the best way to thank her invasive friend.

Nora has found her place in line at another gingerbread-themed bar. Her wine glass is now empty. I seize the opportunity and sidle up next to her and share my theory.

"I've been good this year. For all you know, I could be the guy she plans to set you up with tonight."

Those long black lashes flutter. Hints of freckles show beneath her blush, and I have the oddest craving to place a kiss on the tip of her delectable nose.

"You really never told Anna about us?" The question is left field. It reminds me how stressed she'd been about Anna finding out about us. Her eyelids narrow, partially covering those soulful irises. With that adorable squint, I imagine she's a lie detector personified.

"I told you I wouldn't."

"Thanks. I figured you didn't, but there were a few comments she made. I wondered."

"Why? What did she say?"

"She'd talk about you whoring yourself out to all the nurses. And I wondered if that was Anna's way of warning me off from you."

"Whoa." Okay. How did Anna even know about the hospital? What I did or, more specifically, who I did? Jackson. My brother-in-law. He'd seen one or two of the nurses I'd been with. And a fellow resident. But it was all mutual. Our med school and resident lives didn't make relationships easy. A whore? Talk about harsh.

As if reading my mind, a teasing smile flits across those tempting lips. "All right. She didn't use the word 'whore.'"

"That's the word you applied?" An attractive blush underscores her cheekbones and along the sides of her throat.

"One time she said Jackson had mentioned you seemed to get plenty of action. I'm gonna clear the air now so you don't go strangle Anna."

"Thank you." I express my gratitude with emphasis because that's exactly what I had planned to do.

The bartender winks at her when he slides her now full glass back to her over the bar. She doesn't give any sign she notices, but I do. My arm grazes her lower back as I guide her away from the man.

"There you are. Have you stepped outside yet? On the patio? It's a winter wonderland with snow falling. Olivia's party planning agency did amazing work." Anna's voice comes out of nowhere, and I smoothly remove my arm from Nora and slide my hand into my pants pocket.

"The city skyline is breathtaking," Nora says to Anna. Her comment underscores the jaded New Yorker I've become. I followed Nora through the entire maze, and I didn't notice the skyline. But then again, I'd been focused on a specific posterior view.

"I've only peeked from the doorway. I'm waiting to go out in it." Anna points an index finger at her hair. "My hair will frizz." Jackson stands beside her, assuming the silent husband pose.

"Did Delilah find you?" Nora asks Anna.

"Yes. It's my understanding she's played with the seating arrangement. Heads up," Anna tells her.

"Did she put all the single men at my table?" Nora seems concerned, and Anna laughs. I do not.

"No. But she has someone in mind for you. I think it's a fellow redhead, so…"

"Oh, my god." The tips of Nora's fingers cover her lips. "He's not from Evolve, is he?"

"I'd hope not. Why?" Anna asks.

"There's a guy with red hair in business development. He's nice. But... I'm going to go find Delilah. This is ridiculous. She really shouldn't be trying to—I go on dates. I'll show her my Tinder profile."

I'd like to see her Tinder profile. That would be worth re-activating my account.

"Bad idea. Never show her any of your dating app sites. But yeah, she's kind of got it in her head that you should be with a redhead so you can have redheaded kids," Anna tells her.

The barely-there blush on Nora's skin transforms to a full-on rouge and spreads across her chest, almost down to the curved top of her breasts.

"If I don't see you later, thank you for inviting me. This party is stunning," Nora tells Anna.

With that dismissive note of gratitude, she weaves through the crowd. Her auburn hair bounces, and I squelch the urge to continue following her.

"What table am I seated at?" I ask Anna.

"Mine. You're my brother." Jackson, Anna's husband and therefore my brother-in-law, grins. I will berate him for sharing my personal life with my sister, but with Anna standing right there, I wait. "What if I want to be at Nora's table? How strict are people being? I thought it was buffet style."

"It is, but they assigned table seats. It's hard to ensure people have seats without assigned seating." Anna presses down on my forearm and doesn't speak until I give her my attention. "Nora is a good person, Ashton. She's not someone to take lightly."

On that point, my sister and I agree.

ight years ago

ASHTON

"What's your story? What brings you to New York?" Energy suffused the breath of fresh air before me. She didn't belong in this crappy apartment or this overcrowded city. I imagined she'd be at home on a farm, maybe one with pigs and cows and horses. Twin braids would perfectly frame those oversized brown eyes. She pulled her legs up underneath her and swirled the wine in the plastic cup.

"Typical story. Finished college, wanted to go

into advertising. I applied to agencies in both Chicago and New York."

"Where are you from?"

"Iowa."

"Wouldn't Chicago be a more natural choice?"

"They're both big cities. I don't own a car. Never have. I figured New York would be easier to live in. But, really, maybe New York chose me. The only person who responded to me was a New York City recruiter."

"So, what have you been doing since graduation?"

"Oh, my class will graduate in June. I finished early. That's why I was one of the unfortunate souls looking for a job mid-year. Right at the holidays. I'm so lucky Evolve was hiring."

"And you said you're an art director." I thought about Anna, but I didn't want to bring up my sister. "What do your parents think of you living so far away? In the big bad city?"

She fidgeted with a frayed edge on the bottom of her sweater, and her gaze dropped.

"My mother passed away. I don't know my father."

"How old were you when she passed?" She avoided my gaze, and I understood.

"I was young. But it's not the same as you. I didn't really know her." Her lashes fluttered, and she peeked up at me. An urge to lift her onto my lap and hold her, to tell her she was strong and everything would be okay, came out of nowhere, but I shrugged it down. She didn't need a savior. She'd made it this far on her own.

"Who raised you?" I asked in lieu of touching her. The alcohol loosened her inhibitions, and she shared.

"A lot of people raised me. I was in foster care from age three to eighteen. I don't remember a lot of the earlier families. My last years in high school, I lived with Shonda. She's the best. I owe everything to her. Right now, she has four children staying with her. Social services calls, and if she has room, she always says yes. The woman deserves sainthood."

"She treated you well?" I couldn't help but ask the question, even after her fountain of praise. Maybe I'd seen *Annie* one too many times, but I couldn't fathom anyone taking in so many kids unless all they wanted was money.

"The best." Her teeth sank into her lower lip as she paused. "The state doesn't give enough money to cover the actual cost of a child. She does it out of the goodness of her heart. And it's not easy. The state has so many restrictions. Like you can't leave the state. And you have to be ready at any time for an impromptu social services call. I know sometimes people get a bad idea about foster care, and there are some horror stories out there, but I didn't have anything bad happen to me. I was lucky." Her definition of lucky and mine differed, but I let it drop.

"Are you going home over the holidays?" I inched forward, closer to her.

"No. I don't go home often. She usually has a houseful, and I feel like I'm adding to her burden. Plus, those kids have been through so much transition and upheaval. A stranger showing up and sleeping on the sofa might be nothing to a normal kid, but I always feel like my presence brings anxiety to them because it's yet one more change in their lives." Her emotion rose, building in her throat, and her nostrils flared. "I speak to her on the phone every week. When I was in college, I would send her money when I could, but New York is so expensive, I think it will be a while before I can send her anything."

"Wow." The wooden armrest dug into my lower back. I didn't have any idea what to say or where to direct the conversation, but an admiration for her strength and resilience sprouted.

"Maybe it's just a factor of being in Iowa. You know, a small midwestern town. But the families who took me in were always nice." Sadness tinged her explanation, and I changed the subject.

"Are there as many cornfields out there as they say?"

A relieved smile spread. That smile was like a beam of sunshine. "So many." The light through the window offered a ghostly glow, but a happy vibe enveloped this optimist. "One thing I miss is how clean the air smells. I never thought about it until I arrived here and smelled a city. Back home, a bad smell is, you know, a pile of cow manure. And even that doesn't smell after a while. And it's so open. And the stars. At night, it's breathtaking. Like, really. Every night I used to go out—it's just..." She rambled on, and I saw firsthand her love for her home. In the city, artificial lights snuffed out the stars, and exhaust fumes clouded the streets. I wondered how long it would be before she found her way back to her open fields, clean air, and a sky full of stars.

resent Day

NORA

"ISN'T THIS PLACE INCREDIBLE? I'VE NEVER SEEN SO many trees." Marta, one of my colleagues from account services, holds a martini glass between two fingers. Her eyes hold the magic of a kid at Christmas.

Every year, it seems the friends outdo themselves. An unlimited budget no doubt helps. I've never shared my opinion with Anna or Delilah, but as one of the attendees who'd been at the original event, it seemed to me that the friends had more fun together back when it was really just friends, and before the event blew up to include business relationships.

"I'm so glad I didn't miss this. I seriously thought about leaving earlier today so I'd get the full week away," Marta continues. I sip my drink and smile. My feet aren't throbbing yet, but they're sore.

Pete from Human Resources speaks up. "Nora, is your family here in New York?"

The question isn't an odd one, but I fidget with the stem of my wine glass, and my throat tightens as every single person standing in our little circle stares at me. All of the colleagues standing in my circle know me in a professional kind of way. We do our jobs well together. They know I'm not married, and I don't have kids. I know Pete is married, I know Marta is engaged, but I don't spend my free time with Pete or Marta. I could tell him my parents aren't around, but my answer might beget further questions, and all I really want is to sit down, eat dinner, and then begin my holiday vacation.

So, I fib. "Yes."

"Ah, so that's why every year you offer to hold down the fort."

"It's not a big deal. I'm never needed." I can't count how many times I've offered up this defense.

"Two years ago, didn't you come in to make

adjustments to some newspaper ads that had the incorrect legal warning?" Marta asks.

"Good memory. But it was really nothing." It had actually taken me all day to make the adjustments to the files since it hadn't been my account, and I'd needed to double-check every single aspect of a media buy going out to fifty-two papers across the country. Still, it had been a welcome, calming day. I'd pumped music throughout the studio, something I would've never been able to do on a regular workday.

Pete asks Paul, Marta's fiancé, about one of the baseball teams. That's my trigger to move on to another group. "I'm going to go see if I can find Delilah," I announce to those in the circle standing near me.

"I think I saw her outside," Pete calls after me.

"Great. Thanks." Armed with that piece of valuable intel, I turn in the opposite direction to the open room where they'll soon be serving dinner.

Biding my time, I meander through the faux winter wonderland, surrounded by a bevy of twinkling lights. The words to *I'm Dreaming of a White Christmas* float through the air, and I hum along. I don't recognize any of the other guests in the area adjacent to the banquet room.

"There you are." Tingles alight across my skin. For the past seven parties, he's been absent. Tonight,

I can't get away from him. We stand beside a floor-to-ceiling window broken up by large iron panes.

"Everyone said we had to check out the roof deck. But it's beautiful in here too." Ashton's gaze centers on me, and heat rises all along my cheeks. I scan for a hidden heater, but no, it's the Ashton effect.

"The event planner did an amazing job with the decorations." It's a comment I've heard over and over again. Ashton brushes my arm and directs my attention outside the party to the night sky.

"You can see a couple of stars from here."

"I think one of those is a plane." Sure enough, the bright light shifts much too quickly for it to be anything other than a human invention.

"I think they're going to be announcing dinner soon. Should we head in to find our tables?"

The warmth from his touch on my lower back as he guides me through the maze absorbs my attention. His tuxedo repeatedly brushes my bare arm, and I lean closer rather than away. Up ahead, an enormous trellis wrapped in fir boughs, twinkling lights, and red glittery balls signal the entry to the banquet room. A flurry of fake snow falls over the trellis and the cluster of trees surrounding it. The falling snowflakes, along with the song in the background, tugs at something deep inside, and I pull out my phone to capture the moment. Shonda would love to see this.

"Beautiful," Ashton says from my side. The scene holds a magical quality, what with the thick white flakes and the trees and the city backdrop. I tuck my phone back into my black bag and zip it closed. Ashton's touch warms my arm and is simultaneously comforting and disconcerting. Eight years ago, I'd been young enough to be quickly enamored with his smile and easy confidence. Now, I know better. *Go and find your table.*

He points up. That teasing, flirting smile is back. "Mistletoe."

Sure enough, above us, tiny red berries are intertwined in the familiar green ball, barely noticeable in all the greenery and lights on the trellis.

"That's not supposed to be there." It's not. Delilah told me where she'd placed it. I don't think he cares if it's supposed to be there or not, but I do. My sense of self-preservation kicks in, and I step into the banquet hall.

"It's bad luck if you don't kiss under the mistletoe. Remember?"

ight Years Ago

NORA

"COME HERE."

The only light source came from the narrow window between the bunk beds. A streetlamp lit the sidewalk below, and even though my fifth-floor walkup rose high above it, the streetlight radiated through the glass. Ashton shone like a shadow in front of me. His dark hair is darker, his skin pale.

"I am here." My insides fluttered as nerves fired off. I sensed, rather than saw, what he wanted.

"Come closer." He tugged on my fingers, pulling

me toward him, attempting to close the two-foot gap between us on the futon.

After sharing so much with him, I felt exposed. My one-room apartment didn't have any sense of home to it—rather, it felt like yet another temporary place to stay. Another temporary place to store my stuff and sleep at night. Emotion welled up, and I struggled to shove it down.

He pulled me closer, close enough I breathed in his musky cologne. His body generated heat, a welcome warmth because the steam heat had kicked off, and a chill permeated the area.

"How much have you had to drink?" He plucked a strand of hair and twisted it around a finger, then tucked it behind my ear. The pad of his finger brushed my cheek. We hadn't refilled our plastic cups. But he'd filled those cups up with far more than a restaurant glass of wine. It hadn't been particularly good wine and tasted too syrupy sweet. I'd drunk it fairly quickly, though, and enough of a buzz circulated that I wouldn't drive if I owned a car.

"Huh?" He tilted my chin and lowered his head. His breath brushed past, and a current of energy buzzed.

"Three or four?" I feared he might believe I'd had too much to drink to kiss me, so I added, "Over the course of the whole night."

The room spun a bit. Inviting a strange man up to my apartment ranked as so completely out of character that alcohol most definitely impacted me. I licked my lips and tentatively ran my fingers over my nose as a subtle test. Nope, I could still feel my nose. I wasn't overly drunk. And it was my first weekend in New York City, and I itched to do something crazy and wild.

When I'd set out for the party, being wild hadn't been on my list of things to do, but I'd spent my life walking the line. Always so afraid to act up or to disappoint for fear of being turned over to another family. In college, the fear had translated to a fear of losing my scholarship. And in New York? I had a job and an apartment. Meetings between my social services agent and my foster mom were long gone. There would be no one to report on my errant behavior. No one for an observer to share that I'd been acting out, or I'd made a poor decision.

I leaned forward, inching my lips closer to his, as my heartbeat shot forward in a sprint. My breast pressed against his hard chest, and his lips brushed mine softly. Then he deepened the kiss, and sensations rolled throughout my body, down to my toes.

He tasted of sugary wine with a subtle hint of cinnamon. A dizzying array of swirling lights played behind my eyelids, and I breathed in deeply, gasping for air from the intensity. His hand slid underneath my sweater, onto my bare skin, and goosebumps spread across my arms. My brain stopped functioning, lost in the physical sensations. I tugged on his shirt and matched his movements, allowing my fingers to roam along his bicep, then along his back, and up to his broad shoulders. When I found the base of his neck and his soft hair, my nails scratched along the skin, and he moaned.

His lips worked their way from my earlobe to the sensitive area along my throat. A need surfaced deep in my core. We sat facing each other, but I wanted to straddle him. I wanted closer.

He tugged on the bottom of my sweater. "Can we take this off?"

I answered by lifting it over my head. I wore a basic white support bra, another Goodwill find. There was nothing sexy about it, and the edges held a dingy gray from so much washing. But in the dim light, it didn't look dingy at all. And Ashton pushed me onto my back, seemingly eager to lie between my legs and to get that bra off.

The narrow futon offered little room, and he shifted, letting one leg fall to the floor. He lost his balance as he readjusted himself, attempting to lie over me, and jerked forward. The whole room shifted, and a loud crash reverberated through the apartment. My head slid toward the floor.

"Oh, shit. Are you okay?" he asked. I hung from an unnatural angle, my head inches above the floor. Laughter bubbled up, and once it leaked, I couldn't stop it.

"Oh, my god. My roommates are going to hate me. We broke the futon."

"I have a feeling they neglected to tell you the futon had a broken leg. I didn't move on it that hard." He rubbed a hand over his face. He sounded serious, but his slight smile revealed he, too, found our altered position amusing.

"Yeah, I think they did say they found it on the sidewalk." I pushed up off the broken furniture.

"Ah, a sidewalk find. New York City ritual." A person could leave essentially any unwanted furniture or even absolute junk on the sidewalk, and within an hour, the item would find a new home.

"Should we move to my bed?" If the light had been on, I was certain he would've noticed the ruby red of my burning skin.

He combed his fingers through his hair. I wondered what he was thinking as his gaze traveled from the dilapidated futon to the bunk beds. Did he want to do this?

I'll never know what demon possessed me, but I twisted my arms behind my back and undid the thick bra strap. His gaze fell on me, then centered on my breasts as the bra fell to the floor. The whites of my breasts glowed in the light, and I trembled as I waited for his decision.

"Which bed?" he asked.

I pointed to a lower bunk. He took my hand and led me the five steps to the edge. I backed up onto the mattress, my gaze locked on him. He rested one hand on the rail of the top bunk and shook it hard. The blocks of wood didn't budge.

He unbuttoned his shirt and dropped it to the floor. Then he toed off his shoes, undid his belt buckle, and slid off his pants, including his briefs. His erection stood out, eager and begging. I blinked, astounded we'd progressed so far and unsure what to do next.

"You don't have to if you don't want—"

"No, I do," I interrupted him. I stared at his long, thick erection, and he smirked.

He leaned forward and unbuckled my jeans, and with my help, he removed everything I wore, including my socks. He bent down and picked up his pants and tossed a condom onto the pillow beside my head, then climbed beside me, careful not to bang his head on the top bunk as he did so.

He hesitated. I wrapped my fingers around him, watching his reaction carefully. Searching for instructions and a sign. He groaned and dropped his lips to mine, and he took over.

resent Day

NORA

"It's bad luck if you don't kiss under the mistletoe, remember?" The most infuriating smirk crosses his lips. So damn sexy and attractive. I could totally imagine him as a star in some hospital drama, the unrealistic kind where he'd sometimes wear perfectly fitted jeans and a V-neck tee with a white lab coat and a stethoscope around his neck. It's no wonder, really, that I, and probably half of Manhattan, fell for his schtick.

"What do you say? One kiss to thwart bad luck?"

"That's ridiculous." My cheeks burn, and given my complexion, an inferno on my face means red now overpowers my pale skin. *Lovely.* I scan the party, flustered, searching for a person I recognize.

"Did you know the Celtic Druids believed mistletoe held sacred powers?" Maybe my knowledge of the ancient history will be enough to send him scurrying.

"According to Nordic myth, anyone standing beneath mistletoe deserves not only protection from death but also a kiss." I twist in surprise, and he continues. "And in Victorian England, a wise girl never refused a kiss under the mistletoe." He thinks he's victorious, and he's outmatched my historical knowledge. If he thinks I'm afraid of forsaking a marriage proposal, like the ladies of yore, he's seriously mistaken.

"Are you really going to risk a year of bad luck?" *So, he's back to luck.*

"Here's the thing about luck. You don't know if it's good or bad until you have some perspective. Eight years later, I have perspective." He blinks, looking appropriately shellshocked. "Have a good life, Ashton."

I throw him a confident smile, proud of myself for staying strong. Yes, he is as gorgeous as I remember, but I've been down that path. One thing I learned is that while I might like the packaging, I didn't care for the substance. I push through the crowd into the room where the band had been playing.

Sam Duke, the party's benefactor, stands before a microphone on stage. "Alright, alright, alright," he begins.

A woman I'm passing asks her friend, "Do you think he's a big-time McConaughey fan?"

I can't help but fill her in. "It's whatever movie that's from. He watched it all the time at his frat house."

Her mouth forms an 'oh' shape, and I smile as I move on through the crowd. Olivia, his wife and Anna's best friend, stands to his side, holding a red martini glass. It's clear she adores her husband. The way she's standing near his side, it appears she's going to step in and also speak.

"At the end of every year, the holiday season is the perfect occasion to make memories with the people you care about most. Thank you for joining us to celebrate the season."

As anticipated, Olivia takes a turn at the mic. "This party originated with a group of friends getting together with one tree, one menorah, and a handful of Shrinky Dink ornaments. Over the years, the party has grown. Our friendship circle has grown. And we're forever grateful. Thank you for joining us for our annual Friendsgiving. Food has been served. The banquet room is through the evergreen arch. Enjoy yourselves, and Merry Christmas, Happy Hannukah, Happy Kwanzaa, and Merry Everything."

Couples crowd around the exit doors in the direction of food. I linger behind as sitting through dinner at a table of strangers holds no appeal. And, somewhere out there, Delilah waits to push me into yet another matchmaking attempt.

My feet ache. There's a level of cheeriness and goodwill floating through the air, but I have this sense that it's just out of my reach. You'd think after putting the kibosh on Ashton, I'd be in a better mood, but instead, my mood sinks. All these happy, smiling people only serve to heighten my awareness that, yet again, I do not fit in.

My feet wander against the crowd, out into the massive hall and the skylight and the windows, and to the elevators. I can email thanks to the hosts. They're going to be so overwhelmed with goodbyes at the end of the night that they won't remember if they see me again or not.

The elevator door opens, and I step inside. All I want is to open my apartment door, kick off my shoes, remove my bra, and settle beneath a blanket. I'll light several candles and read. Maybe I'll have a third glass of wine. Nat King Cole belts out a holiday tune in the elevator, and I lean back, closing my eyes.

There's a sadness, or rather, a general lack of gaiety that's impossible to deny. But there's also a growing sense of satisfaction. I didn't enjoy the party, and I left. The action is so unlike me. It's novel. And I like it.

The elevator doors ding, and I exit with a renewed sense of energy. As I hand over my yellow coat check square, the elevator ding echoes in the lobby. I silently wish the coat check person would hurry it up. The young man holds out my black wool coat, and I lift it from his extended arm then bolt for the door without pausing to put it on.

"Nora." Ashton's voice fills the lobby as I push through the revolving doors out onto the sidewalk. I already said my piece.

I charge across the street, toward the corner of a building and a narrow side street. My high heels slip on the smooth, uneven cobblestones. Cavernous black gaps between the pavers present a perilous path. I hop from paver to paver, rushing forward as my senses tingle. He's near. He's close. *This is ridiculous. Just face him.*

My right leg catches, and I lunge forward, palms out. Pain ricochets simultaneously through my palms and my knee.

Fuck.

On hands and knees, in the middle of the road, I rotate my head to the left. Two circles of yellow light increase in size. Two black loafers and the hem of black dress pants step between me and the oncoming headlights.

Ashton raises his arm and waves as if the vehicle might not see a woman and her coat sprawled out over half the street. The car slows to a stop.

"Are you okay?" Ashton asks with his arm still out as if the car might plow us over.

I sit back on my heels and wipe my palms. They burn, and an oily film covers my raw skin, as do minuscule rocks. I hurt. *Fuck, it really hurts.*

Ashton bends down to my eye level.

"What hurts?" *Me.*

He holds my elbow and supports my weight as I gingerly rise. Instinctively, my right leg bends. With a deep breath, I will myself to check it out, expecting blood. I am no longer wearing a shoe. The guilty heel remains a foot back, wedged in a black hole in the street. My knee throbs and pain radiates up my thigh. Under the streetlights, the blood on my knee gleams a dark red, and one lone rivulet of blood streams down my shin. *Gross.*

Rather than fall on the pavement again, I lean on Ashton's offered arm for support. The driver in the stopped vehicle opens his car door. "She okay? You need help?"

Vehicles zoom by on the nearby avenue. I should be able to easily get a cab from the corner.

"Can you stand on your own?" Ashton asks. His question alerts me to the fact I'm still leaning on him.

"Yes." I put my weight on my left leg, then reach to pick up my coat, but Ashton scoops it up in a flash and lifts my broken stiletto from the street. The heel remains intact on the shoe, but it hangs precariously from the base.

I accept the proffered shoe from him, but I'll never wear it again. There's a garbage can beneath the streetlamp, and I'll toss it on the way to the street corner to hail a cab. I hop on my left leg, in my heel, from paver to paver. My foot slips and Ashton latches on to me, one arm circling me from behind, his other arm providing support.

"Let's get you to a bench so we can check out that knee."

"I just need to hail a cab. Or Uber. I'll be fine."

"I'm a doctor. Let me look at it." Ashton's deep timbre brooks no room for discussion.

"I don't think so." I grit out the words, hating my need to lean on him to reach a bench.

ight years ago

NORA

"Where are you going, hot stuff?"

Confused, my eyelids fluttered open. Morning light filtered through the white paper hanging over the single rectangular window. Ashton stood halfway to the door, his back to me. Slowly, he turned and smiled.

"I've got to run. I'll be in touch."

A hoarse question reverberated from above. "Do you have her number?"

"Zoe?" Mortification stunned me. When did she

get home? Had she been on the top bunk the whole night?

"Yeah?" she asked.

"I thought you went home." I covered my eyes with my hand, then mouthed "I'm sorry" to Ashton as he grinned from across the room, inching toward the door but otherwise seemingly unaffected by my roommate's presence.

"Change in plans. He has a nice ass, by the way." Ashton let out a chuckle at Zoe's comment, and I slowly pulled the sheets up to my chin. He stood straighter and shoved one hand into his coat pocket.

"I do need your number. What are you doing Christmas Eve?"

"No plans." He'd been on his way out the door. Why did Zoe say anything?

"Where's your phone?" Ashton asked.

"Over there." I pointed at the far wall. He picked it up off the floor.

"You need to charge it," he offhandedly commented as he tapped on the screen. "Now you have my number too. I'll be in touch."

As the door closed behind him, Zoe called out, "Bye-bye, Loverboy."

"Zoe!" I screeched, then pulled a pillow over my throbbing head. "I can't believe you did that."

"What? Why not? He stayed over. Don't you want him to call?"

"Only if he wants to." The pillow muffled my words.

"Honey, trust me. Loverboy is going to want to. Trust. And now, when he flashes back to your tight hoo-hah, he'll be able to make that booty call. You're gonna thank me for that."

The sinking, heavy sensation in my gut told me that no, I would not be thanking her.

DO YOU WANNA BUILD A SNOWMAN?

resent Day

NORA

PAIN SHOOTS THROUGH MY KNEE AS I DROP ONTO THE black wooden bench near the building entrance. The skin tears further as I bend my leg, and a burning sensation centralizes around the injury. Ashton kneels before me, all doctor. Lines form over his brow as he examines my knee, squinting under the streetlight. The fingers of his left hand trace his right palm. If he had surgical gloves, I imagine this is when he'd put them on.

With his index finger an inch away from the side of my knee, he pauses and asks, "I'm going to touch you now. Is that okay? I need you to tell me if something hurts."

"My knee hurts, but it's fine." I only need a bandage, but I swallow the comment. He's acting like a doctor, and I don't argue with medical professionals.

He gently prods my lower thigh, the knee, calf, ankle, and foot. He presses on the sides of my knee and compares my right knee to my left. I stare at the cars crisscrossing the nearby avenue. His fingers lightly brush the back of my calf and my leg jerks.

"Do you run?" he asks.

"Excuse me?" I blurt. *Why does he care? Why is he here? Why did he follow me?* If it hadn't been for him following me, I wouldn't have rushed on these stupid cobblestones, and I wouldn't be bleeding. He grips my ankle and moves my foot up and down.

"What do you do for exercise?" *Oh. He needs to know for a medical reason.*

"Spin class. Yoga. No, I don't run."

"You'll need to take some time off the bike. Your ankle looks good." He continues touching me, crouched before me like a servant on the sidewalk. His comforting caress on my calf relaxes the taut muscles. He should be back at the party. Sure, he ghosted me, but I don't deserve special treatment. I don't need special treatment for a skinned knee. "But that knee. I need to clean it." Declaration made, he stands. Bereft of his touch, my skin chills. It's cold outside, it's dark, and I'm so ready to end this night.

"An Uber should be here in two minutes." The app glows on my phone screen.

"Let me come back with you. I'll clean it up. If it swells, I can wrap it for you, or at least let you know if I think you should visit an ER."

"I'll be fine." I'm not a kid. I do not need this level of attention.

"You haven't eaten dinner, and I can bring you food."

"Thank you, but I'm good with delivery." *As if I'd ever agree to invite him back to my apartment again. Fool me once...*

"But I can take care of you. And you don't yet know how much pain you might be in. And we can take the time to catch up."

"I'm sure Delilah has someone planned for your table. If you come home with me, then you'll screw up her plans, and some single woman is going to be stuck at a table full of couples." He smirks. It's a semi-smile that shows amusement, and it's absolutely contagious. I feel the smile spread on my face. I work to keep it small. I pretty much lost all semblance of grace and composure in my tumble, but I can attempt to pull off a cool attitude.

"Maybe the single lady at my table will find the single man at yours. Since you're obviously not planning on going back inside."

The thought of Delilah's plans going haywire entertains me, and I grin in spite of myself.

"Does that expression mean you're thinking about it? Because I'd love to help. And I'd love to find out what you've been up to. I've never forgotten you."

The sincerity in those dark eyes cinch my chest, and I find it difficult to swallow. I hadn't forgotten him either. Could that mean something? Was that normal? Of course, it's normal. We hooked up. And he didn't call. But it's been eight years. You never know. Things could be different. We could be different.

A blue Chevy Nova bounces along the cobblestone and stops in front of the street sign labeled Tribeca Rooftop.

"That's my car. If you can wave him down here, it's fine for you to come up. But you don't need to on account of my knee. This is an amazing party. Please don't miss it on my account. And I'm not drinking anymore tonight." I throw in the last bit because if he comes up, he needs to know nothing will happen between the two of us. If he has visions of us sharing a bottle of wine like before and one thing leading to another, I need to clarify that misperception before he wastes his night.

He waves his arm, and the blue vehicle lurches forward, the headlights dropping left then right on the uneven road. He bends beside me, and I loop an arm over his shoulders, expecting to use him as a crutch to get to the car. His arm bends beneath my legs, and when he stands straight, he lifts me into the air. I squeal, shocked. He groans, probably because I'm heavier than he anticipated.

"Put me down!"

"You can't hop on the cobblestone. You'll twist your other ankle." In four long steps, he reaches the car. A buzzing sound emanates from somewhere on his being, but he ignores it, intent on opening the passenger door and assisting me.

He hands me my broken shoe then pulls out his pager. One hand rests on the open passenger door. With an apologetic expression, he drops the pager into his trouser pocket.

"I'm sorry. I'm on call tonight. I've got to go in. When you get home, take a washcloth with warm water and clean that knee up, okay? Put some ice on it, especially if you see any swelling. Text me if there's swelling, okay?"

I don't have his number, but I nod in agreement. I

deleted his contact information from my phone years ago.

He closes the car door, and I hear a soft thud through the roof as his palm slaps the car twice. He charges up the sidewalk to the avenue. The moment he reaches the corner, he raises an arm straight in the air as he scouts the yellow cabs. The Uber driver repeats my address to me. The driver, a nice young woman with her hair pulled back into a low bun, shifts in her seat. "Are you hurt?"

"No. Not really. I fell. It's just a skinned knee. Broken heel." I hold up my red stiletto as evidence. Inexplicable disappointment filters through me. I barely had time to get excited about Ashton coming up to my apartment. It would've been cool to let him see my adult apartment, to see I've grown since the days of four people sharing a studio.

The streetlights and familiar storefronts whizz by through the back window. So much in my life has changed in the last eight years, and so much hasn't. The city, for example. In eight years here, restaurants and small start-up businesses change overnight, but the overall view, the general landscape, hasn't changed at all.

"Was that your boyfriend who put you in the cab?" The woman's voice startles me. I'd almost forgotten another human being sat three feet away.

"No."

"He was hot."

I smile my cordial, polite-response smile. He is a good-looking guy. Too good-looking. And with that thought, relief replaces the disappointment weighing me down. *Saved by a pager.*

ight years ago

ASHTON

"WHAT ARE YOU STILL DOING HERE? I THOUGHT YOUR shift ended an hour ago." Markus, a fellow resident, slid into the booth across from me at the hospital cafeteria. "It's Christmas Eve. I figured you signed up for the early shift so you could spend time with family."

"My sister and I are getting together later. I need to get through three more chapters of infectious disease, and then I'll be on my way."

"It's Christmas Eve! Get outta here." He looked at me like I'd lost my mind. And maybe I had.

Markus's expression had me laughing. But then a vision of the auburn babe from several nights ago crossed my mind. She'd probably be sitting at home alone. On Christmas Eve. I owed her a text. I picked up my phone.

You home?

Anna and I didn't have big plans. Her friend Olivia had invited us up to Connecticut for Christmas dinner. When I asked Anna if she'd be cool with me inviting a friend, she'd been down for it. I'd purposely held back from texting Nora. Since meeting her, my brain kept circling back to that night. To prove to myself I could control the distraction, each day I'd outlined everything I needed to accomplish before I'd allow myself to text her. I set her up as my reward. Only my lists had been too long. In two days' time, I'd yet to earn my reward.

But, as Markus dug into the plate of cafeteria spaghetti, I fingered the corner of the pages of my textbook. Was anyone else really studying on

Christmas Eve? I'd already worked an eight-hour shift.

Yes.

The one-word text came through, and within seconds I tapped back.

Any plans?

She'd told me she didn't have any plans. No one should be alone at Christmas. I slammed my textbook closed as Markus inhaled his dinner.

"I'm outta here."

He grinned, revealing marinara-stained teeth. "That's the spirit!"

Her text came through.

Watching movies.

I dialed Anna and tucked the phone between my ear and shoulder as I packed up my backpack.

"Hey. What time are you planning on coming over?" I asked the moment my sister answered.

"Bobby. Hey. Actually, I was wondering if you'd mind if we didn't get together tonight. Olivia wants me to come up and stay with her. Her boyfriend is being a dick. Would you be super upset if you took the train up to Connecticut by yourself? I can tell her no. But she's upset, and you know she's never happy at her parents' house, and I figured you're probably going to be exhausted anyway and would sleep through the—"

"Anna. It's fine." *Better than fine.* "No worries. I'll see you tomorrow. Text me Olivia's parents' address again so I have it."

"We can pick you up from the station. Just text me which train you catch."

"Will do."

I wished Markus a Merry Christmas and headed out onto the city streets. While I felt pretty sure this time Nora wouldn't have a roommate at home, I contrived how to get her back to my apartment. I had three roommates, but at least we each had our own bedrooms. I hadn't lived in a bunkroom situation since freshman year undergrad. But if I showed up with flowers, then whisked her away, would she come back to my place? Did she even own a television?

 resent Day

NORA

BUZZ. BUZZ.

I peer up from beneath my fuzzy blanket. On my television screen, snow flurries fall over a picturesque New England town and rest in a charming pattern on the heroine's perfectly coiffed blonde locks.

Buzz. Buzz.

I did not order delivery. Unexpected visitors simply do not happen in Manhattan. My phone rests upside down on my coffee table, beside my iPad. I'd intended to snuggle up and read but ended up flicking through the channels and chose to work my way through my movie list. The Hallmark Channel movie on the screen isn't on my TBV list, but the caption said, "Guaranteed to make you smile," so I clicked. I have yet to smile, but forty-five minutes in, I do yearn to move to a small-town movie set.

Buzz. Buzz.

"Jesus. Go away," I mumble to my cave. I toss off my blanket with a huff and shuffle to the off-white plastic box protruding on the wall. My index finger pushes down on the square button, and with my face inches from the box, shout, "Helloooo?" fully prepared to inform the person they have the wrong apartment.

"Nora?"

The deep timbre sounds familiar, but it can't be. My insides squirm. I push the button as I school the riot in my belly. *It's not him.*

"Yes?"

"Do you have plans for today? I texted, but you didn't respond, and I was near your place, so I thought I'd check to see if you might be home."

Since I'd been using my eReader to read, I hadn't really been on my phone. The work email flow had trickled to zero. *He still has your number...*

"Nora?"

"Ashton?" *It can't be...*

"Can I come in?" I stare at the box.

"If he's bothering you, I'll tell him to go." My elderly neighbor's gruff words vibrate through the speaker. William lives directly below me. I wear only socks in my apartment because he can hear every step if I wear shoes, and he doesn't hesitate to complain. I can see him right now, hovering over Ashton, prepared to demand he leave.

My thumb presses the square button, and I shout, "It's okay."

After pressing the buzzer to let him in, I glance down at my outfit. Flannel shorts, a threadbare gray sweatshirt, and giant fuzzy socks that reach midway up my calves. There's no time to change. Besides, he's the one coming by unannounced. I run my fingers through my hair, pull it back into a ponytail, crack my door open, and wait. Footfalls pound on the stairs, growing louder as the seconds pass.

I peer over the railing on the landing. Ashton didn't come alone. A chocolate brown dog trots beside him on a leash and the metal jingles as they climb.

"What are you doing here?" I ask the moment his face comes into view.

"I have the day off. I wanted to check on your knee and see if you felt up to walking around. Maybe going for lunch."

I blink, then another question forms. "How did you know where I lived?"

"I saw your address on the Uber app last night."

"How did you know my unit number?" I didn't put that into the app.

"Your last name is by the buzzer." And so it is. My neck and face warm. *How annoying.* My fingers instinctively cover my throat. "I hope you don't mind. And I have Anna's dog. We can wait out in the hall for you."

The dog's tail curls on the end and wags back and forth. Her pink tongue hangs out as she pants. Chewie's dark brown eyes peer up at me. I recognize the dog from the photos in Anna's office. A dog person by nature, I scratch behind her ears.

"Hello, Chewie. Of course you can come inside." I open the door wide for them to enter ahead of me. "I'm sorry. I'm still in my pajamas. Having a lazy day."

Bells jingle from the den. Ashton stops down my short hall, past the galley kitchen. I close the door and quickly catch up to him.

On-screen, the hero heaves himself between the heroine's thighs, and the muscles on his bare back shine in the light as they flex from the exaggerated on-screen movement. *Kill me now.* It looks like I am watching porn.

I rush to the sofa, lift my blanket, tossing it

around frantically until the remote clatters across the floor. I leap for it. Chewie mistakes it as a game and lunges forward.

Ashton tugs on the leash just as Chewie's paws land flat on my back. On my hands and knees, I grip the remote, aim it at the television, and flick it. The screen flashes to black.

"Well, that's embarrassing," I admit. "Never know what you're going to get with a good old Hallmark movie."

He gives me a skeptical look and points. "That was Hallmark?"

He has a point. "Maybe Netflix."

He grins. We stare at each other, me still flat on my butt, him sky high above me, and it's awkward as all get out.

"I guess your knee is okay."

Ashton offers a hand to help me up from the ground. As soon as he utters the word *knee*, an uncomfortable pang throbs. The thin scab on my knee cracked, and thick gooey blood oozes. *Gross.*

"So, is that the kind of television you like?" I think he's teasing me, but I'm not one hundred percent certain.

Several rebuttals bounce around as potential responses, but I settle on a half eye roll. "It's just a holiday romance."

"Anna likes those kinds of shows, too."

"It's not a show. It's a movie. And they based this one on a book I read."

"Oh? What's it about?"

"Nothing." I wave my hand, embarrassed. There's no way I am sharing a romance plot with him. When you say them out loud, they all sound ridiculous. They are to be appreciated in the heart.

Ashton gestures to the sofa. "Sit there so I can check out your knee."

Beneath the hardened scab fragments, fresh blood oozes. I focus on his hair. It's neatly combed. It's longer near his forehead but not nearly long enough to cover his eyes.

Dr. Daughtridge kneels before me and gently presses along the sides of my knee. "Did you have any swelling?"

"Not that I've noticed."

"How did you sleep?"

"Why?"

"I was wondering how bad the pain was."

"It was fine. I'm fine. Everything's fine." *You don't need to be here.*

"Good. Then you'll be up for going for a walk with me. I was thinking we could walk through the Christmas Village near the public library. I need to do some more holiday shopping. Thought you might help me find a good gift for Anna."

"You're talking about down where all the artists have booths?"

His gaze remains on my thigh. *Is he staring at my knee?* I glance down, half expecting to see gushing blood, but it's the same oozy, broken scab.

"Ashton?"

"Exactly. It's a bit of a walk for us to get to it, so we can take a cab if you're not up for it. But I have a lunch reservation for an outside table. They allow dogs. You up for it?"

Am I up for it? Why is he even here? My comfy sofa calls to me. I can resume my movie whenever I want. But leaving the comfy cocoon of my apartment isn't part of my plans.

"I don't think so. I'm not even dressed."

"If you pull on some jeans and boots, you'll be good to go. Although I do like those shorts." His sexy smirk plays across his lips, and my stomach does the annoying, uncomfortable flip. It's the pre-date flip that I hate, and that is the singular reason I've bowed out on so many dates in the past.

"Why are you here, Ashton?"

"What? It's Christmas week, and we're both alone. No one should be alone over Christmas break. This was Anna's idea."

"Anna told you to come here?" A combination of disbelief and indignation claws at me. He nor Anna should feel responsible for me. I'm fine on my own. They don't need to worry about me.

"Well, no. But she worries about me being alone. She likes the idea of me spending time with someone. I think it eases her guilt for leaving me alone over the holidays."

So, Anna's worry is for Ashton, not me. That realization alleviates some of the festering agitation. While Christmas is not my favorite holiday, I love everything about the Christmas Village in Bryant Park. The varied booths house a variety of artists and craftsmen, and musicians nearby play holiday music. But if I go on my own, I can enjoy it more. Take all the time I want at each booth. I don't need to go with Ashton. And what if I fall for his schtick again? Once he gets what he wants, which I suspect has nothing to do with appeasing Anna, I'll just be the woman who fell for him—twice.

ight years ago

NORA

"MERRY CHRISTMAS."

A rough, unshaven jaw brushed against the sensitive skin along my throat and below my ear in a ticklish yet delightful way. I stretched my body, reveling in the feel of the muscular form behind mine.

My body hummed, content and happy. Christmas Eve night had been daydream-worthy when he showed up at my door...shocked? Stunned? I was all those things and more. When I got those texts, I halfway suspected Zoe had somehow hacked his phone. Last night had been, to use a Zoe-word, amazeballs. And waking up with him the second time around was, well, let's just say, one fantastic yuletide. I didn't remember many truly happy Christmases, and definitely zero Christmas mornings when I woke feeling blissed out.

"Merry Christmas to you." I rolled onto my side so I could more easily press my lips to his throat and along his jaw. My naked body molded to his firm, muscular one.

"I think it's going to be." When he dropped his lips to mine, I discovered I didn't even mind the morning breath. His hands roamed my body and explored. I wantonly spread my legs, giving him access. His finger dipped into my core, and I squeezed my thighs together to show him how much I wanted him. His thumb and his fingers and *oohhhh*.

"Baby, you're wet."

"I'm not surprised." My body buzzed with an unfamiliar energy. I reached between us and wrapped my fingers around his eager erection. He let out a soft groan, and his eyelids flickered closed.

"You're hard."

"I've been hard for at least an hour, pressed up against you. It was all I could do not to wake you."

I grinned. "You did wake me." I stroked him, matching the pace of his finger inside me. "What should we do about this?” I asked, referencing the extremely firm object in my hand. I rubbed the bead of dew that emerged into the head and along its length.

The pad of his thumb circled my mound, and his fingers increased pace. My toes curled as my muscles seized and then relaxed. He kissed my lips, then the tip of my nose.

He stretched for the side table and nabbed a plastic square. He tore it open with his teeth, and with practiced ease, sheathed himself. He settled between my legs and eased inside delectably slowly.

“God, you feel so good. Warm. Tight.” Once seated balls deep, he lifted my leg, placed it against his shoulder, and fell into a natural rhythm. Within minutes, we were sweaty and loud as our skin slapped and the headboard beat against the wall. And then we were just gone. I moaned and chanted until it was all too much, and he released, pulsing inside me, crashing down over me.

He lay on top of me, gasping for air. A thin layer of perspiration coated his chest and his forehead.

Pounding reverberated over his headboard.

“Merry Christmas to you, fucker! Some of us had to work last night.” His roommate’s voice came through the paper-thin wall as clear as if a curtain hung between us. I raised a hand over my eyes in embarrassment, and Ashton chuckled, placed a sloppy kiss on my cheek, then slid out with a low groan.

"Love you, Brandon," he shouted.

"Yeah, yeah. Fuck off," came the grumpy reply.

"I guess having your own bedroom isn't all I thought it would be," I mumbled, hand still shielding my eyes.

"It's fine. I forgot he was here. There's three of us in this apartment and nothing but drywall as room dividers. It happens."

He shrugged like it was nothing. And I immediately felt like I'd entered a fraternity and was just one of the girls who'd agreed to sleep over with one of the brothers. I'd been friends with girls who had experiences like this. I'd never dated a fraternity guy. I'd dated a couple of guys in college, but none that had been into me.

Guys had never been something I excelled at. But these two times with Ashton had me wondering if I'd been missing out. In college, I had just been so scared of slipping up and losing my scholarship. I hadn't dated much at all. I'd thought my friends who sometimes gushed about sex were exaggerating.

Ashton got up and walked out of the bedroom, completely naked with the condom still on.

I heard a male voice yell, "Christ, Ashton."

I pulled the covers up below my chin. The bedroom door remained closed, but the voices in the apartment sounded nearby. I heard bits of conversation.

"Who've you got in there? I thought Barb went home." The comment sucked the oxygen from my lungs, and I strained to hear more.

"She did."

"Nice."

"You are such a fucker." The guy did sound like a jerk.

"Nah, I'm pretty sure that title goes to you. So, who is she?" I never heard the answer.

After about ten minutes, the door reopened. Ashton held two mugs of coffee. Brown liquid sloshed over the side of one while he juggled with the doorknob. He kicked the door closed and set the mugs on the bedside table, then searched the floor and pulled on a pair of boxers. He sat on the edge of the bed, and the mattress slumped with his weight.

"Brandon called dibs on the shower first, but we can get in after him."

"We?" I backed up to the headboard, one hand pressing the comforter over my breasts, the other clutching the coffee as if it was a life force.

"Yeah. We're supposed to be on the train to Connecticut in an hour. We can push it to two hours, but we can't be much later. This family that's having us over for Christmas lunch, I know them, but we aren't close. Anna's close to Olivia, but she's not close to Olivia's parents."

"Wait. What is your sister's name?"

"Anna. Anna Daughtridge. We met at her apartment, remember?" He smirked and reached out to grasp my thigh and squeeze.

"Shit." No way. His brow wrinkled in confusion. "You didn't tell me your sister was Anna. Did you?" I thought back over what we'd said to each other. No, he'd definitely never mentioned her name.

"I don't know. I'm sure I did." He relaxed onto the bed, propping up his head with one hand.

"I'm sure you didn't." My head hit the back of the headboard with a resounding whack. I shifted forward and rubbed the now sore spot.

"What's the matter?" he asked.

"Anna is my boss."

"So?"

My eyes had to have bugged out. "That's not okay. I've worked there for one week."

"From what I can tell, people within the agency date each other all the time. Olivia's dating a guy who works with her at her agency."

"Who is Olivia? I've worked there less than a week. I don't know many names."

"Oh. Olivia works for a different ad agency. I can't remember the name. She's tall, with dark hair. She's Anna's roommate. Her boyfriend was there.

European-looking guy. I think he's an ass. I don't know everyone who was there that night. I can't believe they had so many people packed into that small apartment."

I hooked up with my boss's brother. Who does that? She could fire me. She definitely won't think much of me. She might even know this Barb person. Holy shit. I let myself drink, and look what happens. I'm screwed.

"What color do you call your eyes?" His question pulled me out of my head.

"Hazel. Sometimes they look green, or brownish, sometimes bluish." I paused then asked, "I bet they're green right now, aren't they?"

"Yeah, more or less."

"That's because I'm freaking out." He had to help me out here.

"Why?"

"Because I don't want anyone thinking I'm loose or that... I hooked up with my boss's brother." Saying the words out loud did not improve the situation. "This is not okay."

"First, I'd hardly call that a work party. It was a selection of people Anna and Olivia invited over to their place. Second, no one cares."

"I do." Frustration at his casual manner over this potentially enormous issue strangled me, making it hard for me to swallow, and I shoved off the bed, searching for my clothes. He leaned back against the headboard, kicking his legs out and crossing his feet. His phone vibrated on the bedside table, and he picked it up.

"Merry Christmas...Yes, I'm getting ready...I'm thinking the eleven o'clock train?" He raised one eyebrow, waiting for me to agree to his estimated timing. I'd packed last night when he coaxed me into staying the night with him.

I shook my head and mouthed the word "No."

"Twelve, maybe?" he asked tentatively.

"I can't go with you," I whisper-shouted.

When he hung up, he cocked his head and studied me. The second my head appeared through the hole in my sweater, he said, "She's not going to care."

"No. No. She can't know. I mean, maybe once I've been working there for a while. But please. Please. I can't go with you. I can't. That's not the impression I want to make on my boss."

"You realize this is just Anna, right? She's, like, two years older than you."

"She's still my boss. And she's my first boss after college in a real job. This job matters. Please. You don't understand what it's like for women. I don't want to be known as that."

"As what?" He smirked. He knew, of course, what I was talking about.

"You know." I threw stray clothes into the shoulder bag.

"Fine. You don't have to come to lunch. It'll probably blow, anyway. Olivia's family is really uptight."

"Who is Barb?" I shouldn't have asked. I had no business asking. My skin crawled as I asked. I wasn't the jealous type. I had nothing to be jealous of. But how could I not ask?

"You heard Brandon?"

I tugged on my socks and focused on getting the seam correct against my toes as I nodded my answer.

"She's nobody. A nurse I hook up…or hooked up with a few times."

"Cool." I had no business getting upset. I'd just met him. And at least he didn't turn around and tell me she was his girlfriend. He tugged on my fingers and pulled me up against him.

"Don't be jealous. She's no one. Especially now that I've met you."

resent Day

NORA

"I DON'T THINK SO. YOU SHOULD HAVE CALLED BEFORE coming all the way over." He should leave. The best course of action will involve him leaving.

"Not a big deal. Had to take the hound for a walk. You don't live far away. I doubt you realize it, but you actually live quite close to Sloan Memorial, where I work. And you weren't responding to text… remember? And…I had a feeling I might need to work a little harder this time around to get you to go out with me." He sounds so smooth and collected. It's borderline nauseating. *I am smarter than this.*

"This time around? We never really went out before." The apartment heat has kicked in. I didn't hear the telltale steam heat noise, but it had to have kicked in because it's so hot I am fanning myself.

"No. But we should have. I've always felt bad for not calling." He tilts his head as he looks down at me. He looks sinfully good in his casual outfit of faded jeans and a button-down shirt. But he's always looked good. *I appreciate the apology...no, wait, was that even an apology?*

"It was fine. It was a long time ago." I hold the frame of the door, swinging it slightly, prepared to close it and put this whole weird journey down Christmas past behind me.

He cocks his head and chews on his lip. His warm gaze increases my discomfort, and I stare down at his barely worn running shoes.

"I don't buy it. If it was fine, and such a long time ago, you'd come out with me. It's a gorgeous day. A little chilly, but not bad. And a cold front is headed our way. You know, doctors advise getting out of the house for at least thirty minutes each day. Come on out, stretch that leg, get some fresh air, and have lunch with me. Prove to me you're fine." *Seriously?* "Prove to me that your eyes are often green, and it's not just me that brings the green out."

That sexy, insanely attractive smile comes out, and I bend down in spite of the pain in my knee to scratch Chewie. I need to breathe and think. Ashton leans against the wall, and every time I glance up, he looks so good I drop my gaze. Minutes pass with me scratching Anna's dog. Some of those minutes, my brain is working, and some of those minutes, it's like it's fallen into a candy-induced coma.

"Please. I really would like to spend some time with you." *Gah! Just go.* "Please?"

"I do love Bryant Park at Christmas. That's where you're talking about going, right?"

"Yes."

"But I'm not going to ice skate." *Where did that come from? He didn't even mention ice skating.*

"I'm positive they don't allow dogs on the ice. You're safe."

"Okay. So, I'll just go get dressed."

"I'll wait out here. No rush."

Through the closed door, I hear him fussing at Chewie with a repeated "Get down, Chu."

After the third time, I crack open my bedroom door. "It's okay. She can sit there."

She looks at Ashton with an expression that says, "Told you so."

From behind the closed door, I call, "Do you watch Chewie a lot?"

"A fair amount. I'm beginning to suspect Anna

doesn't like me being alone, and she's assigned her dog to keep me company."

Dressed, I open the door. I am wearing faded blue jeans and a fluffy white sweater with snow boots. Unable to do anything with my hair, I braided it into two low ponytails. He gives me a look that makes me feel like I'm a snow bunny…the sexy kind. My insides fizz. There is something about his heated gaze that has me suspecting he'd rather stay right here, push me up against the wall, and do something else entirely. Or maybe that's simply me projecting. Which means we need to get out of here, stat.

"Do you ski?" he asks. *Okay, he's clearly not having the same thoughts I'm having.*

"No. Never. Let me get my pocketbook, and I'll be ready to go."

"Anna, Jackson, and I go up to Vermont sometimes. You should come with us. You'd have fun."

"Oh, I don't think so. I think last night I proved my lack of coordination is legendary."

"You were in five-inch heels on cobblestone. I'd bet I could get you skiing in no time. About once a year, Olivia's husband, Sam, flies a group of us out to his place in Aspen."

"I know. I always see the pictures." Delilah and Anna love those trips.

"Why haven't you ever joined us?" I've considered

going. But I don't ski. And a free trip to Aspen feels like too much. I don't want to owe anyone. And I've always thought it would be all couples. I've never known Ashton was joining until after the fact when they've shared trip photos.

"Just hasn't worked out," I tell him.

"Next time, you should go. It's gorgeous out there. Sam's place is stunning. He's this co-founder of an internet start-up, but I guess you already know that. Anyway, they have some more advanced slopes, but they also have some good beginner areas too."

I transfer my wallet from my black leather pocketbook to a cloth bag I can comfortably wear across my shoulder and check the inside pocket for tissue and Chapstick. Satisfied, I zip it back and ask, "Ready?"

He helps me with my coat and scarf. When I grab my mittens from a basket, he says, "You won't need those. It's not that cold."

With a shrug, I drop them into the bucket. "Okay."

True to his word, he hails a cab after we exit my building, and the three of us climb into the back seat. Chewie insists on sitting by a window, which puts Ashton and me beside each other.

"I swear, Anna does not train that dog."

"She loves her. There are more pictures of Chewie in her office than of Jackson."

"And don't you find something a little wrong with that?"

I bark out a laugh. "No. Do you have any pets of your own?"

"No. My hours aren't really conducive to it. Although I somehow survive when I'm on dog-sitting duty. But it's a lot of work. Maybe that's why I'm Anna's first choice. She's trying to prove to me I can take on more than plants. What about you? I didn't see any signs of a pet. Was there a cat hiding?"

"No. I had a cat several years ago. But one of my roommates let it out, and I never found it. Which, in the city…"

"I get it. You know, your eye color has now transitioned to a bluer shade. With brown around the edges. That's the shade I remembered." I look out the window, away from him.

"I like to think someone found my cat and took him into their apartment. I put out fliers everywhere, but you know, people don't always read those." I hate thinking about what might have happened to Vixen. "The experience proved a pet with unreliable roommates doesn't work."

"But you don't have roommates now."

"No. I've had this place for a little less than a year. I've thought about it, but I guess, like you, I'm not sure about my schedule. I work a lot."

"Is Anna a slavedriver?"

"No. She's not at all. I love working for your sister. But I'm also helping the biz dev team. It can get busy. And I volunteer a lot, so…"

"Where do you volunteer?"

"At Crossroads. It's a soup kitchen. It's kind of in midtown, on the east side. I've been doing it for years."

"That's nice of you." I focus on the view out the window as the cab zips down to Bryant Park.

The blue skies above are a rarity in the haze of winter. All the store windows are decked out in a holiday theme, and holiday balls, wreaths, and garlands hang from the streetlights. Even without the Hollywood effect of falling snow, I believe deep in my soul no place feels more Christmassy than New York City.

The cab lets us off on the corner of 41st and 6th. Ashton tugs hard on Chewie's leash to prevent her from bounding away uncontrollably. The crowds on the sidewalk are thick in this area of the city, as tourists intermingle with city residents, all wanting to visit the Bryant Park shop booths.

"I read they have over sixty booths this year," I tell Ashton.

"Have you ever been ice skating here?"

"I've never been ice skating. Period."

"You know, I'm beginning to think there are

quite a few firsts you and I can share." He flashes me that sexy smirk. He's attractive. Yes. But it's what's underneath that matters. People can change, but has he? "You up for trying new things?"

"I'm not that daring." He's teasing and all about the fun, but my words are quiet and serious. I have never been the kid who put herself in danger. No one else looked out for me, so I had to.

As we approach the maze of white-covered booths, the crowd forces us to separate. Ashton keeps Chewie close to his side. The dog wags her tail, thrilled to be smelling all around, and she looks up to every human passing, silently begging for attention.

There's a booth overflowing with handknit scarves, hats, and mittens. My fingers flutter over the soft material of an angora scarf, and I tell him, "Feel this." He complies.

"Soft," he says.

We weave in and out of the booths, pointing at paintings or pottery we like. A ball of mistletoe hangs over the doorway of one booth. Ashton points up, and I smile but pick up my pace.

In one booth, a fluffy stuffed teddy bear made of alpaca catches my eye, and he waits outside for me to purchase the item. When I exit the booth, he asks, "You like stuffed animals?"

"It's not for me. There's a woman from the soup kitchen with the most adorable daughter. I think she'll love this."

"That's sweet. Is she a volunteer?"

"No. She's fallen on hard times. Her daughter is in foster care. She eats at the soup kitchen to save money. In order to get her daughter back, she has to afford housing, and she's saving. It's tough."

"That sounds—they take your kid if you can't afford a home?"

"No. It's not like that. It's…they placed her daughter in foster care because she had a drug problem. She's been in rehab, and she's doing good. But the state can't give her daughter back until she has a roof over her head, you know? She's on a waitlist for a state-subsidized apartment, but that can take forever. So, every dollar she earns, she's saving."

"How old is her daughter?"

"Four."

"How old were you when you went into foster care?"

Surprise that he remembers filters through, but then again, how many women has he dated who have been in the foster care system? My background doesn't count as one of the ways I want to stand out in other people's minds, but I can't change it.

"Four," I tell him, then duck into a booth filled with hand-hewn knives. I trace the beautifully carved wooden handles, paying far more attention than normal to knives. When I exit the booth, confident enough time has passed that the conversation topic will change, Ashton holds a phone to his ear. While I've been studying knives, he has morphed into Dr. Daughtridge. He listens intently, covering his other ear with his hand to better hear.

"Right. I'll come in." He hangs up and runs his fingers through his now unruly hair. "Nora. I'm so sorry. That was the hospital. A patient I operated on a week ago is having some issues, and he's back in the ER. I need to go check on him."

"Hey, it's okay. No worries," I say. My chest is lighter.

"Can you take Chewie?" Unsure I heard him right, I pause, waiting for him to clarify. He grimaces. "I know it's a lot to ask, but I need to get up there."

I sense his concern, see it in the faint lines around the edges of his eyes and his frown. Whatever is going on with his patient is serious, probably a matter of life and death. "Of course. I'll walk her back up through the park, and she'll be good and tired."

"I'll come back to pick her up later." Ashton's

long strides place him five steps ahead of us when he glances back and calls, "I promise."

I smile my polite smile. I don't doubt he'll be in touch to claim his sister's dog. But I can't help doubting everything else about him.

$\mathcal{E}$ight years ago

NORA

"WHAT'VE WE GOTTA DO TO TURN THAT FROWN UPSIDE down?"

Delilah pushed a venti concoction my way. Our desks faced each other, but Delilah came around to my chair and bent over me, a look of concern plastered on her face.

"I'm not frowning."

"Yeah, right. You've been moping around this whole week. You even made me stop playing holiday music. What's up, girl?"

"It's past Christmas. Tons of people—in fact, most people—are done with the holiday music. We've had it shoved down our throats for months."

"Maybe." Delilah sat her ass on my desk and crossed her legs. "But you seem especially down. And moody. Did you not have a wonderful holiday?"

I thought about that loaded question. I'd had a great Christmas morning, full of promise. I'd been so hopeful. And then it unfurled. Would it have been different if I'd just agreed to go with him on Christmas Day? Would I have had a somewhat normal Christmas, admittedly a lunch with a family I didn't know, but then maybe dinner with a gorgeous guy? Was he pissed I didn't go with him? Or did Barb come back into town?

"What is that face? I know something is wrong." Delilah wasn't the officemate who stayed on her side of the proverbial fence.

"It's nothing, really. There was a guy I hooked up with. And he didn't call. It just sucks."

"Really? What guy? When? Tell me everything."

"There's really nothing to tell."

"When did this hook-up happen? Where? I want details. Who is this guy?"

"Does any of that matter if he hasn't called me?" I dropped my yellow number two pencil, and it rolled toward my phone.

"How long has it been?"

"Two weeks."

"Hmm. Asshole. So, you know what that means?"

"What?"

"We're going out after work."

"What?"

"Yep. Best way to get over a guy is to get under a new one. And I have just the place to go. Tons of twenty-somethings. Drinks on me."

There was no point in fighting Delilah. She was a force. And a part of me welcomed the idea of going out with a friend and doing something other than watching my phone for a text or call. The pain of the wait was excruciating. And I hated being all girly. I hated hoping. I hated being disappointed. I hated putting myself in that position because I knew better. I promised myself I'd only have two drinks. Clearly, I didn't make healthy decisions if I allowed myself more.

resent Day

NORA

THE THRONGS ON 59TH STREET HUDDLE IN overcoats, wool jackets, and scarves. The heavy clop of horses' hooves and the occasional whiff of raw horse manure blend into the high-pitched jingles of the Salvation Army bells. A jolly, bearded Santa in costume takes photos on the corner of 5th Avenue with a line two or three families deep.

Anna's furry dog strains against the leash to get closer to the horse-drawn carriages, and I scout the wall for the first park entrance to get the unruly dog off the busy thoroughfare. I backtrack to the 59th and 5th entrance near the Pulitzer Fountain, not caring that the east side entrance is out of the way.

Once we bypass the fountain and reach the black asphalt path, Chewie calms down and falls into place beside me. Rollerbladers and bikers zoom along the street up ahead. The trees are bare, and dry brown leaves litter the ground, but under the clear sky, an energy fills the park. It is a weekday, but in Manhattan, any day of the week at any time of day can be busy. This is Christmas week. Many in the city have off work, and combined with an abundance of tourists, Central Park is humming with energy.

The phone in my coat pocket vibrates, and I answer while bracing back onto my heels to prevent Chewie from lunging at a passing jogger.

"Hello?"

"Hey, girl! Merry Christmas! What're you up to?"

"Delilah? Where are you?" She should've left already.

"I'm back home. In New Orleans. But I wanted to let you know I have a little something coming your way. And you are not to open it until Christmas. You hear me?"

"We've already exchanged gifts."

"Yes, but everybody needs something to open on Christmas." Every year, Delilah does this, and once upon a time, I'd hated it. The office does a secret Santa, and then several of our girlfriends get together and do an additional secret Santa, which is supposed to represent a gift to each person. However, every single year, ever since Delilah learned I didn't go home for Christmas because I didn't have family, she'd violated all the agreements and sent a special gift to be opened on Christmas. This year, though, I had prepared. A present sits safely with the doorman in her building, awaiting her return home.

"I'll keep an eye out for it. And you have something waiting for you when you get back," I tell her.

"I love you, babe. Wish we would be back for Christmas so we could have Christmas dinner with you."

"I know. But when I drink a glass of vino, I'll toast to you."

"Oh, here's an idea. We'll Zoom you in for dinner," Delilah says, as upbeat as ever.

"No." My answer is immediate. Joining in on other people's private moments is painful enough in person. I could only imagine the nightmare on Zoom.

"Yes. That's what we'll do. I'll send you dinner!"

"Dee, that sounds like hell to me." I cut to the

chase, knowing it's the only way to cut her off at the pass.

"Oh, well, fine. Offer stands. Why're you panting? What're you doing?"

"I'm out walking."

"Exercise. That's good. Fantastic. Get those endorphins pumping."

"How's everything down there?"

"Something is up with you. I know that tone."

"Delilah. What are you talking about?"

"You don't sound happy. Your tone drops deeper, just a touch above a baritone when something's wrong. And your plan was to vegetate on the sofa in the seclusion of your apartment for days. Why are you out walking?"

"If I told you, you wouldn't believe it."

"You're training for a marathon?" Her question earns a laugh.

"By walking? No. Hold on." As I lift a discarded wrapper that Chewie seemed intent on eating and toss it in a nearby trashcan, I debate telling her. At this point in time, my friendship with both Anna and Delilah is cemented. Eight years ago, keeping secrets mattered. Now, there's zero point.

"Do you remember the guy I hooked up with years ago who never called?"

"Hm. I don't really remember you hooking up with… refresh."

"When I first started working at Evolve. Right after Christmas, someone ghosted me. And you made it your mission to get me under someone else?"

"It sounds vaguely familiar. I don't remember the guy at all, though."

"Well, you wouldn't. You never met him, and he never called."

"Yeah, I wouldn't remember that. It's not like it's that rare. Hell, I used to do that to guys. So, this guy from ages past didn't call, and what? He called you, and you're walking to meet him right now?"

"Close. I'm walking his dog. I met him for lunch, only he had an emergency call to the hospital, and he left his dog with me."

"Well, you definitely know you'll see him again this time. How'd you guys reconnect?"

"At the party."

"Wait? The holiday party? You didn't stay for dinner. I had someone at your table for you. Did you leave with this guy? Oh, my god. Spill!"

"I didn't leave with the guy. But we reconnected at the party."

"And?"

"We went walking around Bryant Park. He's a surgeon. One of his patients returned to the ER. He got called in. That's it."

"A surgeon, huh? I wonder if Anna's brother

knows him. What kind of surgeon? We could get Bobby to check up on him and see what his story is."

"You mean Ashton."

"Yeah, whatever. I know him as Bobby. I can't change people's names in my head on the fly."

"I'm fairly certain you've had around eight years to adjust."

"I'll text Anna, and she'll be—"

"No!"

"Huh?"

"Delilah, the guy is Ashton—or Bobby. Whatever you want to call him. I met him at the first annual Chrismukkah party in Anna and Olivia's apartment."

"You sneaky dog. Why didn't you tell me?"

"Because I was new. I didn't know you well. And I didn't want you guys thinking badly of me."

"Nora? Seriously? After all you've seen us do over the years? You were one of my bridesmaids."

"We hooked up ages ago. No big deal. Why would I mention it?"

"Now that I think about it, you do always go quiet when Anna mentions Bobby…"

"Ashton. And no, I don't."

"So, should I tell you now that I had you guys seated at the dinner table together? He's the guy I hand-selected to hook up with you. And I had mistletoe hanging at multiple juncture points around the table to maximize the chances of you two making a mistletoe connection."

"You had so much mistletoe everyone ignored it."

"Eh, maybe. But I think you're overlooking one important point. My matchmaking skills. I called it."

"You didn't call anything."

"Did he ask you out that night?"

"No."

"Well, then, how—"

"He showed up at my apartment building. It turns out we live two blocks away from each other."

"Oh, my my, my. This is so awesome." A loud "mommy" carries through the line.

"Hun, I have to go. Apparently, the Christmas cookies have cooled, and it's time to decorate them. Oh, Mylanta! This is so awesome."

"No. It's not."

"I've got to run."

"Don't tell Anna." *Click.* The line disconnects before I can explain. I don't care about telling Delilah, but I don't know how Ashton would feel about Anna knowing.

I stare at the phone in my hand, wondering if Delilah heard me before hanging up. I can't risk it, so send a follow-up text.

Don't tell Anna!

BY THE TIME I SLIP MY KEY INTO MY APARTMENT door, I've determined that no, at this juncture, it doesn't really matter if Anna knows. My position within Evolve is cemented and available as long as I want it. Maybe Anna will think twice before making an offhand update about her brother in front of me, but other than that, she's not going to care. It's ancient history. We were so young. I doubt she'd even mention it to Ashton.

Chewie trots beside me up the stairs, leading the way by about a foot or two as my steps slow with each progressive flight. No one cares about something that happened so long ago, except for me. I care. It hurt. Yes, I'd been naive. But I'd thought I found someone in a big, new city—and he disappeared. As a kid, I'd been through it. I'd transition between foster homes, where one family would take me on for a year or two, and then I'd move to the next one. And they'd swear they'd keep in touch. But everyone gets busy.

Heart heavy, I collapse on my apartment sofa. Chewie sniffs around the edges of my apartment, tail wagging.

"Shit. She needs water," I announce to the empty apartment. I find a somewhat deep bowl and fill it with water and set it on the floor. I don't own any dog food.

"Let's hope Ashton isn't at the hospital too long." I open my refrigerator door. I've never owned a dog. "I wonder if you can eat cheese." She wags her tail. *Yeah, I bet you'll eat cheese if I give it to you.*

I turn on the television to the cooking show *Nailed It.* The show almost always makes me laugh and holds zero drama. But, as a contestant's cake collapses in on itself, the humor doesn't register. Nicole, the show's host, belts out her jolly laugh, thoroughly entertained by the catastrophe, and my eyelids grow heavy.

A rapping on my door startles me. I glance at the time. I must've fallen asleep. Hours have passed. Chewie lunges repeatedly, her front paws drumming against the wooden door. The dog's deep bark reverberates through the apartment, and the thump on my floor informs me she's too loud.

"Sshhhh," I admonish Chewie and fling the door open.

Ashton stands in the hallway. He's in running shoes, scrub pants, and his wool winter jacket.

"I'm so sorry. Has she been a terror?"

"Chewie? No, she's been good. She's been laying here sleeping."

"Good. She's mellowed out. When she was younger...Let's just say I had visions of needing to replace your furniture."

"Nah. She's been a good girl." The dog in question wags her curly tail, happy to see Ashton. She rubs her nose in his palm, and when he doesn't immediately pet, she augments her request with a paw against his leg.

"So, I need to head home and shower. I just wanted to get her out of your hair as soon as possible."

"Really, no worries." I locate the leash and hand it to Ashton.

"Can I take you out to dinner since lunch was a bomb?"

"Oh, don't worry about it. How's your patient?"

His expression grows grim. "I had to do a repair. He ignored instructions and busted his stitches. But I think overall he's okay."

"And now he'll be in the hospital over Christmas?"

"Yes, but at least he's alive. So, dinner? I can swing by and get you at six?"

"I don't think so, Ashton. But thank you." I need to close the door on this. On him and all the swirling emotions that unsettle me. Sure, it's ancient history, but it's a history I'd rather not repeat.

"It's because I didn't call last time. Right?"

Buying time to respond, I focus on Chewie, scratching her ears. I prefer being alone over waiting to see if someone will call. I don't like repeatedly checking my phone. I don't like the nerves that prod me from deep within before I go out on dates.

"I always meant to call." He sounds sincere, and I lift my gaze to his, curious if his expression matches the level of sincerity in his tone. It does. "But I was so swamped. Between med school and residency, I barely had time to breathe. And Anna, she didn't really want me to go out with you. And I hadn't decided how to deal with that. And then the next thing I knew, a month had gone by, and it felt like too much time. But that doesn't mean I didn't think about you. Or that I forgot you."

His thumb gently presses against my chin and caresses along my cheek. *Wait. Anna knew?* All these years, she'd known and had dropped cavalier comments about her brother without thinking. Perhaps it was just all so inconsequential to her that she didn't think about it.

"Can I please take you to dinner?" He asks a sincere question, so I ask one in return.

"Anna knew?"

resent Day

NORA

"MERRY CHRISTMAS TO YOU." I UTTER THE HOLIDAY greeting, or some version of it, hundreds of times on repeat. A mild headache surfaces by the time I scrape the last of the mashed potatoes from the stainless steel serving bin. Area restaurants donate generous amounts of food, many clearing out their kitchens before closing for the holiday. Several area chefs and line cooks volunteer time, and the Christmas lunch we'd served smelled delicious. Definitely a level above what we normally serve at the soup kitchen.

Hunger pains jab, but I ignore them. My kind of hunger doesn't come close to what these people experience. I scarfed down a Clif bar and had an extra-large jug of coffee before coming in to help prepare Christmas lunch at Crossroads.

"Hey, why don't you go take a break?" Carlos, the head of this entire volunteer operation, asks. "You've been working for hours."

I wipe my gloves on my now filthy white apron tied around my waist. The line has dwindled. The only items not yet claimed are, unsurprisingly, vegetables. I toss my rubber gloves in the garbage and wash my hands under ice-cold water in front of the stainless steel trough.

Beyond the cafeteria line, grateful families, and many, many loners, dine along the long banquet tables, digging into the holiday feast. Cheerful holiday music plays faintly over the speakers. None of the people in this room planned to be in a position where they had to hunt out a free Christmas meal, but all seem extremely grateful for the option.

"Now it's time to clean up, right?" I ask Carlos as I dry my hands. I hope we are now past our open hours because we are now out of the good food, and I don't want to disappoint if someone comes through the door. I definitely don't want to be the one turning anyone away. Back-up peanut butter and jelly sandwiches sit in a box behind the counter. We've been handing them out along with bananas and apples and donated chocolate banana loaves—all food for later.

"We've got an extra shift of volunteers for clean-up. You've done your duty for the day. Get out of here and go enjoy your Christmas." In all the years I've volunteered at Crossroads, Carlos has never asked me about my family. It strikes me as odd he assumes I have a place to be. After all, as head of the operation, he spends his days surrounded by people with disjointed or nonexistent families and, for whatever reasons, no one to share the holiday. But I am a volunteer. He's never served me on the other side of the cafeteria line, so I suppose that's why he assumes.

A little girl with frizzy hair and freckles below her eyes and over her nose peers over the stainless steel rails. The girl strains on tiptoes, too short to see the food on display.

"Reese, can I help you?" The little girl and her mother, Taylor, visit each Sunday after services. It's a treat to see her on Christmas.

"Do you have any more snowmen cookies?" I wish I had a dozen of the donated cookies to give her. But we ran out of the beautifully decorated cookies before we'd run out of turkey and ham.

"I'm so sorry. I don't." The little girl's crestfallen

expression cuts to the quick. "Wait. Where are you sitting?"

She points to the back, and her mother, Taylor, waves.

"Go sit with your mother. I think I just remembered where one might be." The little girl's eyes light up, and she smiles wide. I untie my apron and drop it in the laundry bin.

"Where are you going to get her a cookie?" Carlos asks with a grin.

"Well, I was thinking Starbucks, but they'll be closed. But maybe the deli?"

"Closed. Everything is closed on Christmas. But… you are in luck. In my office, on my desk, is a shrink-wrapped Christmas cookie from Starbucks. Someone dropped it off with a gift card for me. Go get it."

"Are you sure?"

"It's been sitting there for two weeks. I go for salty, not sweet. I assume since it's shrink-wrapped, it's still good. That little girl won't care if it's stale."

I glance over at Taylor and Reese, then hurry down the hall to Carlos's office. The cookie lies on the side of his desk, near a jar of pens. A light layer of dust has settled over the plastic, and I wipe it against my jeans until it shines.

"Here you go. Will this work?"

She beams like a tiny sun ray. "Mommy, look. I told you they might have extras."

I nervously scan the room, thankful their table set us off from the others, and no other kids are seated nearby. If any other kids ask, I'll be empty-handed.

"Thank you, Nora. What do you say, Reese?"

"Thank you." She wraps her tiny arms around my thigh, then takes the cookie and rocks it in her arms like a baby doll.

"Are you not going to eat it?" I ask.

"No. It's too pretty."

I sit down at the bench across from them and watch Reese. She's adorable. Her mother watches, too, and there's so much love in her eyes that it's heartwarming.

"How are you doing, Taylor?" Taylor's plate remains somewhat full of food. Her daughter's plate is mostly empty.

"I'm good. I got to have an unsupervised visit with my daughter today. It's my Christmas wish come true."

"That's great. And you're doing good?" I study Taylor the way I always do, looking for signs of a relapse. She suffers from an addiction to meth, the same drug my mother succumbed to so many years ago. Like Reese, I spent my youth in foster homes, hoping my mother would win the battle against her demon.

Looking at Reese, lost in her own little world playing with a sugar cookie as if it were a toy, you'd never know, though. She seems genuinely happy. But deep within my bones, I feel the emotion twirling around the girl because those memories still live in me. I know how badly she wishes her own mother could come and tuck her in each night.

"She loved your gift this morning. So much," Taylor mouths to me. "Thank you. Carlos gave it to me. She thinks it's from Santa." I'd known he'd be sure to see her, so I'd left the teddy bear from the park with him.

"My pleasure."

"I wouldn't let her bring it out. It's too nice," she says softly. "Do you think she'll ever forgive me?" Her eyes glisten with emotion. I place a hand over hers and squeeze.

"She will. And even if she feels anger one day, she'll always feel love too." Taylor smiles at me, then at her little girl. She loves her daughter, of that I have no doubt. But addiction is a powerful foe. "Your NA meetings? They're going well?"

Taylor removes her hand from mine. "They're good. Almost a year clean. I have a court date next month. If I can find a place to live, there's a chance I'll get Reese back at the hearing."

"Where are you on the waitlist?"

"Who knows?" I recognize the defeatist position of the shoulders. But I can't blame her. Navigating the housing authority could make anyone feel helpless. And the state can't relinquish custody of a child unless the parent can provide shelter. For someone like Taylor, bringing herself back up from literally nothing and with a felony record to boot, the challenge could feel insurmountable.

"Don't give up. You've got this. Day by day." I repeat the mantra I found to be most helpful. Months weighed like a mountain. When one has to move a mountain, one begins with individual stones. "Take it day by day, and before you know it, you'll have a home, and you'll have Reese back."

As I say the words, I think of my mother. She'd never been able to stay clean. She'd come so close, or so the court records showed. And then she'd slip until one day she slipped too far. But by then, I'd been thirteen years old. Few families wanted to adopt a thirteen-year-old. So, I'd become a lifer. I graduated from the foster care system and became an independent adult on my eighteenth birthday.

As I watch Reese on the bench, I wonder if I'd been like her when I was her age— thrilled with sugar cookies. A lot of my childhood memories were hazy or nonexistent. I remembered the nights the most.

After leaving the center, I stroll mindlessly through the city. Almost all the stores are closed and dark, although many offer lighted holiday displays in the shop windows. The song from the *Elf on the Shelf* movie plays in my head, the refrain "Christmas is the time for forgiving" in childlike voices on a loop. The kids at my last foster home watched the movie nonstop. I hadn't seen it in years, but the song the twins sing under the tree when the elf comes back plays in my head's soundtrack at the strangest times.

Cars whizz by, no doubt in transit to visit loved ones. I huddle under my coat, arms wrapped around me to keep out the cold. Was my mom like Taylor? Struggling with both an addiction and fighting the courts, trying to get her daughter back. Getting turned down right and left because no one wanted to hire a felon or a drug addict. I'd gone through my angry phase.

Over the years, I thought about it less and less. Or so I like to think. But doesn't the past stay with you forever? The past isn't an organ that can be removed. Sure, at thirty years old, I'd created a new life for myself. But had I let anything go? Apparently not, as in those brief minutes, watching Reese, familiar emotions swelled. The familiar ache of missing my mother, of wishing for a different reality, and another sensation I'd grown to hate, the sense of being alone. And if I'm honest, I expected Taylor to fail. I hoped she wouldn't, but a part of me expected it.

My mother had certainly failed over and over again. Seventeen years ago, she failed epically. And for seventeen years, probably longer, I've held on to anger, disappointment, sorrow, and regret. None of those were good emotions. Holding on to them only served to weigh me down. And why? I couldn't change the past any more than my mother could. Hating her didn't hurt my mother. She was dead. No, holding on to hate only hurt me. But do I hate her? No, the emotion is anger. Twisted hurt and pain. But why hold on to it?

Let it go. It's time to pull a princess move and let that shit go.

The ins and outs of my mother's life will always be a mystery. How she came to be so addicted to a drug that caused clear physical destruction would always be a question. Because I'd never hear her story. I had to believe she'd been like Taylor. That she hadn't wanted to become addicted, and maybe no matter how desperately she wanted to get her act together, she just wasn't strong enough to overcome it. No matter how hard she tried, she couldn't slay her demon. She paid with her life and with my childhood. I stop and stare up at the green Jones Street sign. There's a green wreath with an oversized, glittery red bow on it. "I forgive you."

As I round the corner, I feel light. Like I dropped a heavy weight from my shoulders. I physically feel different. Like Christmas magic has sprinkled over me, as if an elf flew overhead and waved a wand, and nearby a chorus of elves sing and cheer.

"I like seeing that smile." The words draw me out of my elf-filled fantasy. Ashton sits on the bench outside my apartment building. His cheeks and the tip of his nose are ruddy pink.

"Are you waiting for me?"

"For a couple of hours," he admits. "Once again, you weren't responding to texts. I remembered you saying that you volunteer on Christmas, but I couldn't remember where. So, I figured you'd finish at some point. It's a beautiful day. Cold, but nice. No harm in waiting."

"You're insane. It's thirty-eight degrees outside."

"Well, I should've worn gloves."

"What are you doing here?"

"I wanted to wish you a Merry Christmas."

"You couldn't have said that in a text?" I bet I have several texts from friends wishing Merry Christmas. I finger the apartment keys in my pocket, not about to take them out or move to my door because then I would feel obligated to invite him up, out of the cold.

"I did say it in a text. But I also wanted to invite you to Christmas dinner. Anna and Jackson are driving back today, and they're having me over. I'd like for you to join us."

"That's very kind of you, but—"

"And," Ashton interrupts me, holding his index finger out in the air to hush me, "I have one Christmas wish this year. And it's that you'll forgive me. I should have called."

What an interesting choice of words. Forgive.

"I don't hold that against you." Obviously, I hold it against him, but eight years later, it's ridiculous I'm holding on to it.

Ashton cocks his head to the side, those dark eyes silently calling bullshit.

"Anymore. I don't hold that against you anymore," I amend.

"Good. Then come to dinner with us. Anna says they bogged the car down with food from Jackson's parents, and it just so happens I ordered a Christmas meal which serves four to six, so all combined, we have way too much food for just the three of us. And Anna would love to see you. If you check your text, I believe there's a text from Anna inviting you."

"Ashton…" I grit my teeth, searching for a justifiable reason to say no. It's a holiday dinner, with a family, and…

"Do you have your phone with you?"

"I forgot my phone. It's in the apartment."

"Ah. Your hesitancy made me worry you'd already read all of our texts."

"No. I'm really okay with the past. Let bygones be bygones and all that." I force a smile to convince him.

"But you're still not sure about Christmas dinner?" He squints, and I open my mouth to explain, but he says, "Would you believe me if I told you I'm different now? It's not that I was a bad guy eight years ago, but my head wasn't in a relationship space. Med school was all-encompassing. One thing I can promise you, this time if I say I'm going to call, I will."

"I believe you." A flutter of nerves contradicts my statement, but I breathe through the jitters.

"So, you'll join us for Christmas dinner? It'll be casual. Just the four of us."

ROCKIN' AROUND THE CHRISTMAS TREE

resent Day

NORA

FOR CHRISTMAS, ANNA'S BUILDING GAVE THE doorman off. The outside doors are locked, and only those with a key can enter. Ashton, of course, owns a key to his sister's apartment, and he jiggles it in the lock until it clicks, and he pushes the door open. Chewie prances, tail wagging, eager to go home.

I have been to Anna's a few times in the past. Once she had me over for dinner on their outside roof deck. I'd also brought a few things from the office by one time when Anna had been down and out with the flu. Jackson had come to the door, and I'd passed the items through the opening as he kept his distance, afraid of transmitting the virus.

In eight years of working together, I haven't been invited to Anna's often, but such is life. We were friends, but she was also my boss. And the boss title remained present in my mind at all times. Delilah, who is my equal at work, feels more like a genuine friend to me. Of course, she's also friends with Anna. Delilah has no problem blurring lines between professional and personal relationships. I suppose being independently wealthy helps to trivialize such lines, as she doesn't depend on her income to survive.

Yet, here I am, entering the lobby of Anna's building on Christmas Day. Her apartment building is small, but it's gorgeous. Her rooftop deck is unforgettable. In my apartment, I have a small fire escape off the kitchen window.

"Thank you for joining us tonight." Ashton's formal word choice does nothing to quell my nerves.

I stare straight ahead at the stainless steel panel. The metal doesn't shine, and therefore only the shapes of our outlines are reflected.

"Are you nervous?" he asks.

"It's dinner at my boss's house," I admit with a

shrug. As a doctor, he probably reads patients all day long. There's no point in lying to him. The elevator doors open, and we step into a hall. The only apartment in this hall is Anna and Jackson's.

"After eight years, I wouldn't think she'd feel so much like a boss. Does my little sister play hardball?"

"No, not at all. I told you. She's friendly. Supportive." But nothing is ever permanent, so I work extremely hard. I never give Anna a reason to do anything but give me exemplary performance reviews. Choosing to stay in Anna's group didn't hurt my career track because when she got promoted, they promoted me into Anna's spot. And now I nurture aspiring art directors and copywriters on my team, much the way Anna did for me.

Ashton raps his knuckle against the door then steps back, in line with me. Heat from entering the warm building envelops me, and I wish I had a hand free so I could tug off the itchy scarf around my neck. I refuse to meet his gaze. Instead, I zero in on the tiny silver circle in the middle of the door. My palms clam up, and my stomach is queasy. My annoying internal voice scolds. *Nervous because of Anna? Seriously. Your nerves are haywire because of the man beside you.*

The door swings open, and Anna greets us with a loud, "Merry Christmas!"

"Hey, sis. Merry Christmas to you." Anna moves to hug me, but Chewie lunges forward, and her paws land squarely on Anna's thighs.

"Oh, and your dog wants to come home," Ashton adds.

"Chu, Merry Christmas, baby dog. How's my baby? Was Uncle Ashton good to you?"

"Does Jackson know you talk to your dog like that?"

The door opens wider, and in a deep, disapproving tenor, Jackson answers, "Yes. I'm aware. Come on in."

"How was your drive home?"

"Easy. No traffic anywhere. Christmas Day is a great day to make the drive."

"It's amazing we didn't get a ticket," Anna scolds her husband with a frown, lightened by a hint of humor.

She lifts the bags of food from me and leads the way down the long, narrow hall to where the space opens up into the living and kitchen area.

"It's too cold to go out on the roof deck, even with the heaters. So, we'll have dinner here, if that's okay."

A gorgeous real tree reigns near the fireplace, with white Christmas lights twinkling, and beneath the limbs, a few wrapped presents remain on the red flannel skirt. *They're going to exchange family presents.*

I've been a part of families exchanging presents for years. It isn't my favorite thing to watch. It is probably one reason I turn down invitations to join folks on Christmas. A twinge of regret for agreeing to come pokes at me. If I hadn't come, I'd be curled up on the sofa, maybe with the television turned to a fire film complete with crackling sounds, and I'd have a good cabernet, a book, and a blanket.

"Can I get you something to drink?" Jackson directs the question to both Ashton and me. I hesitate, waiting to follow Ashton's lead.

"I brought some wine. We can open it and let it air," he says.

"Your sister already beat you to it. We have cabernet decanting. Would you like some of that?"

"Sure." Ashton lightly touches my back. "That okay with you?"

"Yes. Can I help with anything?" I ask, but Jackson points to the sofa, directing us to sit.

"You two get settled. I'll be in with the drinks in a minute. We have some news to share."

In the last month, rumors had swirled around the agency that Anna might be interviewing. On a normal day, she is a happy, smiling woman. But she'd seemed especially exuberant just now. Glowing, even. Would she be giddy over a new position? Would she tell us here, on Christmas?

When Jackson hands me my wine glass, I can't

bring myself to drink it. My thumb glides along the smooth glass neck, up and down. The cool surface and the repetitive movement soothe. It's impossible to follow what Ashton and Jackson are saying.

Anna sits down in a big cozy chair to the side of the sofa, and Jackson moves to perch on the wide slope of the arm of the chair. His hand falls to her shoulder, and she looks up to him. Yes, she definitely glows. It's as if she dabbed on too much blush. Then my gaze falls to the glass of water in Anna's hand. My stomach clenches.

Ashton relaxes back into the corner of his sofa and crosses one ankle over his knee. An easy smile crosses his features. He's figured it out, too.

"I'm pregnant." Anna beams, looking first to Ashton, then to me, her excitement evident. "We told Jackson's parents first."

"Congratulations, you two. So, I'm finally going to become an uncle, huh? I mean, to a homo sapiens."

"Yes, you are!" Anna's white teeth flash, and her hand settles over her still flat stomach.

"If you're lucky, you might get promoted from dog sitter to babysitter," she chides.

Ashton casts a glance over to the aging dog, sprawled out on the hardwood floor in front of the dog bed, not in it.

"Well, cheers." He holds his glass up in the air,

then gets up out of his chair to clink glasses with both Jackson and Anna. The clinks of glass spring me into action, and I push my glass against theirs.

"Now, you can't say anything to the others in the office," Anna warns me. "Not yet."

"Are you planning on leaving?" I blurt the question, and Jackson's startled expression informs me my question is out of line.

"What? No." Anna responds quickly.

Jackson gives a low chuckle and adds, "As if."

"No. But I need to discuss maternity plans. If it's okay with you, I'm hoping to recommend you to cover for me while I'm out, and we'll look at how to cover some of your work."

Instantaneous relief courses through me. You'd think I'd be good with change, given I had so much of it as a kid, but in reality, I don't like it at all. I like consistency. If things are good, why change?

"Whatever you need," I reassure Anna. "I'm there for you. Just let me know." Covering for her meant she would return. Helping to keep things running smoothly while she's out is the least I can do for her.

"Thank you. It makes it easier knowing I'll be stepping out on maternity leave with you in my place."

"As long as you return," I can't stop myself from adding.

"You guys planning on staying in the city, or you going to escape to the 'burbs like everyone else?" Jackson sips his wine. Ashton's casual stance shows he doesn't really care how they answer. I imagine his question is a completely normal one. Life in the city with a stroller and kid entrapments isn't an easy one. Or so I've heard.

"Jackson's been looking at places in both Brooklyn and on the Jersey side. But I'd rather not have a long commute. I'm leaning toward converting my office to a nursery. We have time. I'm not due for another six months. And I don't want you to freak out, Nora, but I am hoping to take a minimum of six months maternity leave."

"As long as you promise to come back, take as long as you want," I say the words with conviction. As long as she's not leaving for good, then I'm good.

"You know, you may want longer than six months, sis. And it's not like you have to work." I sense Jackson fully agrees with Ashton but isn't about to go up against his wife.

"That's what everyone says. That you don't know what's going to happen until you have the baby. But six months is far longer than almost anyone else in our agency has taken. We'll see." I feel Anna's gaze on me as I run my thumb up and down the stem of the glass.

Something dings in the kitchen, and Jackson

hops up to handle it. Anna leans forward, closer to me. She taps my leg, and I stop examining the glass.

"Hey, our friendship extends beyond the office. Even if one of us didn't work there, we'd still be friends."

"Oh, I know," I say. My eyes burn. I'm probably tired. I force a smile.

Ashton calls out from behind the kitchen counter, "If it's okay with you guys, we've set up the food in the kitchen buffet style. Come on in and help yourself."

Throughout dinner, Ashton watches me closely. I can feel his gaze, the same way I felt Anna's. Beneath the table, I rub my thumb across my palm. An old self-soothing habit I learned long ago. Ashton drapes an arm over the back of my chair. I sit up straighter and force my palms flat on my legs. Within a minute or two, he readjusts and places his elbows on the table.

"So, Nora, Ashton told us you were volunteering at Crossroads today. How long have you been volunteering there?" The question comes from Jackson.

"Oh, I'm not sure. Five or six years?"

Anna jumps into the conversation then, asking questions. I explain my role, and the conversation evolves into other charity groups and then a new restaurant that Jackson recommends.

After dinner, the four of us crowd into the kitchen. Anna directs me to be a guest, telling me they'll take care of it all. The space is a tight fit for all four of us, so I tell them I need to call someone and climb the stairs to the roof deck.

146

resent Day

ASHTON

I WATCH HER LEAVE, WONDERING WHO SHE NEEDS TO call. She said she doesn't have a family. Is she dating someone? She'd been alone at the party. But I never asked if she had a boyfriend. But surely, if she is seeing someone else, she would've told me. I'd been more than upfront about my interest in her. As I run Anna's Christmas china under the running water, I remember once again that it's Christmas. There are any number of people she could need to call.

Friends, distant relatives, the list of contacts could be long.

"You seem to like her." Anna's question breaks me out of my trance.

"I do," I answer honestly and pass a plate to Jackson for the dishwasher.

"Then ask her out." Anna playfully shoves my arm.

"I thought you didn't want me dating your employee."

"You're a different guy now than you were back then. And I didn't know her. She was really just an employee. And not just any employee. My first direct report."

"And now?"

"Now she's a friend I'll be in touch with for the rest of my life. She's more of an equal at work than a subordinate."

"I'm surprised you didn't ask Delilah to cover for you." While I could tell she liked Nora, she was clearly closer to Delilah. They vacationed together.

"Seriously?" Anna scoffs. "She's out of the office at five p.m. sharp. She's all about the kids and family right now. She's not about to take on more."

"But Nora?"

"Never bats an eye. I think she'd live at the office if we let her."

"Career woman, huh?" As a Type A, career man, I understand the mentality. Or maybe it's a drive.

"Yes and no. She's independent. But I think she could use someone in her life. Plenty of guys at the office have asked her out, and she's shut them down. Don't think that just because you ask, she'll say yes."

I remembered her yeses. Not that I'd ever share that with Anna. Besides, my sister is correct that the shapely redhead isn't a guaranteed yes. I screwed up before, and she has given no indication she will give me another chance.

With the three of us cleaning, we finish quickly. Jackson and Anna cuddle together on one end of the sofa. Anna leans against her husband, and he rubs her belly. He places a soft kiss on her temple. It's a cozy scene with the roaring fire and twinkling tree.

"I'm going to go check on Nora." I don't wait for either of them to respond. I am four steps up when Anna calls out, "There's a mistletoe hanging beneath the lights I've strung. It's near the table and chairs. Just a small cluster."

"Thanks for the heads up." If I had dated Nora long ago, Anna would've ultimately supported me. It's just, all those years ago, that Christmas Day at Olivia's, when I mentioned the girl I'd met at her holiday party to Anna, she gave me a reason to not push myself outside of my comfort zone. And back then, when I felt so stretched, trying to fit someone into my life didn't feel possible. Hell, maybe it wouldn't have been possible. And med school wasn't nearly as demanding as surgical residency.

Out on the roof deck, Nora stands by the railing, looking out over the city. At the sound of the door opening, she turns her head, but seeing it is only me, she looks back over the vast array of twinkling lights. We are high above most of the noise, but the faint sound of automobiles on streets below filters up above in comforting cacophony.

"Everything okay up here?" Her cheeks are wet, and her arms are crossed. "What's wrong?"

She sniffles then swipes below her eyes.

"Nothing. I just spoke to Shonda, my foster mom."

"Did she have bad news?"

"No. I just realized how much I miss her. And that I haven't been doing a good job of keeping in touch. She has two new kids staying with her now. Another set of siblings."

"She must be a remarkable person to keep taking in kids."

"No doubt." She's shivering. I assume it's from the cold, so I step behind her and pull her back to my chest. "She should get a medal. It can't be easy."

"Does she adopt these kids?"

"No. Most of them find their way back to at least one parent. It's difficult for the state to terminate parental rights. And, even then, adoption isn't always straightforward. She could have theoretically adopted me, but I came to her so late, it was better for me to not be adopted. Coming from foster care helped me qualify for a full academic scholarship."

"They give out academic scholarships to kids in foster care?"

"Well, not everyone. But there are some grants that are set up specifically for children from foster care." Her focus remains out over the city. Her arms are wrapped around herself, and from this angle, I see it for what it is—she's hugging herself. Her thumb strokes her upper arm, back and forth.

"Adoption is a piece of paper. I'm sure she loves you like her own. Like you clearly love her."

She presses her lips together. I hesitate, unsure. She could push me away. But she needs someone. I wrap my arms around her, folding my arms over hers. She shifts forward, away from me, and I calm her with a low shhh, the same way I would a scared child.

"You're cold. Body heat will warm you. I'd give you my jacket, but I didn't bring one up."

Her muscles relax against me as she leans against my chest.

"It's beautiful out here. They're lucky to have a deck like this," she says.

"I think it's one reason they're reluctant to move."

"One?"

"Anna loves the city. She's wanted to move here for as long as I can remember. When she was a little girl, all her posters were of New York City skylines. And *Friends*, you know, the TV show?"

"She doesn't have to leave," Nora states the obvious.

"No. They don't. Plenty of people stay. And they might."

"What about you?" The question perplexes me. Why would my sister having a child require I move? *No, she's asking about your plans.*

"Well, it's easier for me to be near the hospital. I think I'm probably bound to the city."

"Did you have posters of the city on your wall?" *Oh...that's where she was going with that question.*

"No." My childhood room brings back fond memories. "I didn't bother with posters. I let my mom decorate. I was into model rockets, fish, lizards, Legos. What about you? Was the city your dream?"

I can only see the side of her face, but I swear my heart connects with hers as I hold her, and I feel pain. Not a physical pain, exactly, but an emotional weight. I tighten my hold around her.

"The city wasn't my dream, per se," she finally says. "I've never cared about the where. But tonight, when I was talking to Shonda, I realized something." She pauses, and I rest my chin on the top of her head, waiting for her to continue. "Shonda is my family. I haven't been treating her like it, but she is."

"How have you been treating her?"

"Oh, not badly. I just haven't called as much as I should. I haven't visited as often, not wanting to inconvenience her because she's so busy. But I need to get better about that. As much as I love her, she loves me."

"I'm pretty sure every single kid out there goes through some phase where they don't call as much as they should. If my parents were alive, as much as I miss them, I can guarantee you they wouldn't hear from me as much as they should."

"I guess that's one of the nice things about Christmas, huh? It brings all the families together. Forces people to reach out."

"Yeah. Everything slows down. Gives us the chance to think about what's important. Who's important. I'm grateful I have my sister. I don't like that she feels responsible for me, but if she were alone, I'd be the same way. It's good to have someone out there. Biological or chosen, it doesn't matter which."

"What do you mean by responsible for you?" She twists in my arms to better see me.

"She left Jackson's family and drove six hours on

Christmas Day so I wouldn't be alone. I'd say that's juggling some responsibility."

"Well, it's not fun to be alone at Christmas. But you don't have to have someone physically near you. I swear, that phone call with Shonda, I felt her… I feel her all around me."

"I'm sure your call meant the world to her."

"She never gets angry at me. Or holds anything against me. I think I could go years without calling her, and she'd forgive me."

"That's love. She loves you," I tell her. *Doesn't she get that?*

"She does." She taps my arm, and I take it to mean she is ready for me to let go. "We should go back downstairs."

"First," I hold her in place, "you said you forgive me?"

"What do you mean?"

"You forgive me for eight years ago. What I did and didn't do."

"I already told you. It's ages ago. In the past. No worries." She gives me a tiny smile, and her chin tilts up.

"Good. Are you brave enough to risk dating me a second time? Giving me a second chance?"

"We never really dated before." She returns her gaze to the city.

"No, but I'm asking for a second chance. Will you go out on a date with me?"

I stand there. Waiting for her verdict. After a long minute, she pats my forearm and pushes away.

"Sure. Everyone deserves a second chance. We should head downstairs." Her sightline falls to the ground.

I reach for her hand and gesture above us. "Mistletoe."

"We're not under it," she says, still smiling. But this time, her eyes twinkle under the moonlight, and I sense her mirth.

"We're close enough." My thumb grazes her chin. Under the night sky, I can't quite see the shade of those hazel eyes. The space between us closes as she rises and I bend. My breath catches in my throat as our lips touch. She laces her fingers behind my neck and lifts on her toes. Our kiss deepens, and I feel her everywhere. She tastes like gumdrops and everything sweet. Our kiss is a present, and as we break apart, I hope for more. Her lips are swollen, we're both breathless, and she lets out a "wow." I bury my nose in her gorgeous auburn hair and breathe in gingerbread and hints of cinnamon and vanilla. She is sweet, spicy, and tempting. And she is giving me a second chance. Nora is Christmas redemption personified.

resent Day

ASHTON

MY HAND FALLS TO NORA'S LOWER BACK AS WE descend the stairs. The movement is the most natural thing in the world. It's a crazy thought, but it's conceivable the Earth tilted ever so slightly off its axis, and now, with us together, corrected course. The chandelier hanging above the stairwell cast a halo-like glow over her deep auburn hair, and I love the view.

Silently, we enter the den, and Jackson greets us

with a finger over his lips. The firelight dances in the chimney, and Anna lies on the sofa, her head in his lap, sleeping.

"Is it cold outside?" Jackson asks in a low, hushed tone.

"No, not bad," I answer. The scene before us makes it clear our night here has concluded. "We're going to head out," I mouth.

"Thank you for everything." Nora mimics me, her words a whisper.

As we exit into the hall after gathering our coats, as soon as the door closes behind us, she says, "I do believe we just left the most picturesque Christmas evening scene in America."

I raise an eyebrow, questioning her statement as I press the elevator button.

"They just looked so happy and peaceful." The elevator dings. "Imagine how different next year will be for them. This year, they didn't have any toys or stockings. But next year, they'll have a child. And that newborn baby won't care at all for the hoopla, but I bet they deck it out for his or her first Christmas." A small smile flickers across her face as she envisions their future. "I suppose they'll wait a few years before they buy an Elf on the Shelf."

"They'll be sleepless. And probably hosting Jackson's parents and sister. Or they'll be living outside of the city," I say. If my sister moves out of the city, I'll be fine with it. I'll still see her. But I wouldn't see her as often. Still, I wouldn't hold any of life's changes back from her. She deserves a full life. We've been through a lot, the two of us.

"Do you really think they'll move?" Nora asks.

"I don't know. I guess it depends on how hard Anna finds life in the city with a kid. I know Jackson would love to move. He's not wired for the city. Not for the long haul. He wants his kids to have a yard and a regular neighborhood—like he did." His parents still live in the same house where he grew up in Virginia, and when I visited, he'd given me the tour of his little corner of the world, complete with pointing out his elementary, middle, and high schools and the baseball diamond where he'd once hit a home run.

"Have you guys talked about it?"

"No. But he's talked about his childhood. He's like a brother at this point since he's been with Anna for so long. I just expect that's what he'd want. His business partner, Sam, and he are good friends. Sam and his wife, Olivia, you know her, right?" She nods. "They moved out of the city years ago. He still has his place in the city, but they use it more like a hotel when he has to stay over. I wouldn't be surprised if Anna and Jackson move up their way. Anna mentioned she likes Nyack. It sounds like a great area." Way too far from the city for me to commute, but Sam and Jackson both had the kind of jobs that working remotely was possible.

"That's a hike for a commute, right?"

"If you're not doing it five days a week, it's doable. And it's a nice life for the kids."

The elevator opens into the lobby, and we step out.

"It's still early. Any chance I can convince you to come over to my place? I have a Christmas tree with lights. And I make the best hot chocolate." I hold my breath, nervous I'm pushing too hard by asking. But I don't want our evening to end. Or maybe it's that I want our future to begin right this second.

"Do you have marshmallows?" I swear those hazel eyes twinkle with a hint of green under the lights.

"I do. Whipped cream too. And several options to spike it as well."

"Oh, no. I've already had plenty to drink." Her cheerful smile is laced with a joke, and I suspect she's thinking of the night we met. "But nonalcoholic hot chocolate sounds perfect."

I open the door wide for her to exit the building then hustle to the curb, searching for a cab. The number of cabs working on Christmas night ranks low, but luck registers on our side and an available yellow taxi slows to a stop.

I didn't own a tree until yesterday. I bought it on my way home from the hospital. It had been one of the few remaining at the stand near my apartment, and I could tell the man selling them wanted nothing more than to rid himself of his remaining inventory so he could go about his own holiday. I stopped in the deli on the corner of my block and bought the remaining lights they had in stock. There were no decorations, but at night the lights decorating my five-foot-tall tree sparkled. I hoped it would offer sufficient festive flair to my otherwise standard, white-walled New York apartment.

When we arrive at my place, we climb the stairs to the fourth floor, and I hold the door open wide. I'd left the lights on all day, a holdover tradition, as Mom had always insisted the lights stay on from Christmas morning until late Christmas night.

"Feel free to look around. It's not much. Bedrooms are down that way." I enter my kitchen, which is right by the door, and open a top cabinet to locate the pot for hot chocolate.

"Bedrooms? Plural?" Her eyes widen, surprise evident.

"I bought this place as an investment. And, I wanted space for a home office. But before you get too impressed, the second bedroom is closer to the size of a walk-in closet than an actual bedroom." Manhattan real estate is astronomical. I understand her wonder. I rented apartments for years in med school, but once I had a solid monthly income, I invested some of the money I inherited from my parents in real estate. Renting had always felt like I was just burning money each month.

"I like it, Ashton. It's beautiful. I like the high ceilings and these windows." She peers out one window that overlooks Central Park.

"It works." I stir the milk and set a top on the pan, then set about opening cabinets, searching for the hot chocolate mix I buried away.

"It's gorgeous. Really. I can't even imagine living with a view of the park. When I walk by, I always wonder what the people who live along this street are like."

At night, Central Park is dark, but lampposts light the shadows with golden warmth, and the city buildings and flickering lights create a spectacular background. She stands, her back to me, taking in the scene, while she fingers a tree limb.

"So, you're a multicolored lights kind of guy?" she asks.

"I'm a 'you'll take what you get' kind of guy. I bought the lights from the deli. I'm lucky they had any at all." I locate the box of hot chocolate and search for a stamped expiration date. "I normally don't buy a tree. But I hoped you'd come over, and I wanted to have a tree. Thought I might need to use it to lure you up."

I can't see her expression, but I hope she understands I'm joking. Yes, I want her up here, in my home. Yes, I'm hoping things progress with us. But she's not a game to me. I'm not looking to bait her.

She abandons the tree and comes to stand next to the breakfast bar. She watches as I pour the thick hot chocolate into mugs then spray out whipped cream.

"What color lights do you prefer?" I ask.

"I gave up on Christmas trees. Such a hassle to bring up the stairs. And I don't have storage for an artificial one year-round."

"But you had twinkling white lights at your apartment. Is that how you would decorate a tree if you had one?"

"I don't know." She pulls out a stool, sits, and rests her chin on her hands on the bar. "I like color. I like homemade decorations mixed in with meaningful decorations, you know, ornaments that represent memories. And candles. I love the warmth of candles." Her expression shifts to what I might describe as melancholy. I push the hot chocolate her way. She doesn't look any older than when I first met her, but she seems more worldly. Before, with a single glance, you could tell she wasn't a city girl. Now she's a New Yorker. And part of that means she's tougher, or I suppose she's always been tough, but now there's a hardness to her. The city can do that. I suppose life does that. She lifts her chin after sipping the hot chocolate, and a touch of whipped cream remains on her upper lip. I wipe it away with my thumb and get lost in those gorgeous chameleon eyes.

"Thank you for spending Christmas with me." I mean it. Earlier in the day, when I'd sat in front of her apartment building, I'd been aware it was borderline stalkerish behavior. But it was Christmas. I didn't want her spending it alone. And I wanted to see her.

"Our second Christmas together." She lifts the mug in the gesture of a toast but pulls it back before we clink.

"Well, last time, we started the day out together. This time, we're ending the day together. Who knows, maybe next year, we'll finally get to do both, start and end the day together." *And do all the other stuff too.* I glance at my tree in front of the window and imagine it with decorations. Maybe this will be the year I buy a random ornament in July. Mom always did that kind of thing. Somewhere we had a box of those ornaments. Anna and I still needed to go through that box and split them up. Anna had bugged me several times over the years, but I'd never felt the need. Maybe I'd agree to go through the box with her and lay claim to some ornaments, so one day my kids would have a few of the ornaments I'd made as a kid or that I'd helped Mom pick out. After all, surely Anna didn't want the Captain America from our Universal Studios trip or the Chewbacca from Disney. Then again, her dog was named Chewbacca. She might want that one.

Nora sips her drink while I watch her. A touch of whipped cream settles again onto her lip, and once again, I reach out. She has natural beauty. She's wearing makeup. I can see the mascara on her lashes and her eyeshadow, but she wears little of it. Her style reminds me of Anna's. I have no intention of pushing her for anything tonight, but I don't like having this counter between us. She sets the hot chocolate down in front of her.

"Is it good?" I ask.

She nods.

I call out to the room, "Alexa, play holiday music."

Frank Sinatra's sultry voice singing *I've Got My Love to Keep Me Warm* fills the room.

"Would you like to dance?" I stand and offer my hand in a formal gesture. My action earns her soft, sensuous smile.

I lead the way, guiding her in a small circle in

front of my multi-colored Christmas tree. She rests her hands on my shoulders, and mine fall to her waist. We dance in a tight circle, and my heart rate kicks up a notch. There's an energy humming between us. We slow to a rhythm completely independent of the music, and her hands rise along my shoulders to my neck. The track transitions to *I'm Dreaming of a White Christmas* as my lips find hers. She tastes sweet, like whipped cream and chocolate. Her soft curves meld against mine, and I want nothing more than to simply usher her back to the bedroom. *Not this time. It's your second chance. Do it right.*

The song ends, and I step up to the fireplace and flip the switch on the side of the mantel. The fireplace flicks to life, with yellow and orange flames lapping high above the scarcely discernible blue flames. I pick up a throw and set it on the ground before the Christmas tree and the fireplace.

"Want to sit?"

Yes, the sofa is more comfortable. She glances at it, but I move to the floor. Sitting in front of the fire is romantic, right? No one would ever claim I excel at romance. If I tell Anna about this tomorrow and she calls me a goon, it wouldn't surprise me at all. Beneath the single throw, the floor is hard. I get two thick blankets from the closet and create an area for us as she unzips her heeled boots.

"You don't mind if I take off my shoes, do you? If we're hanging out on the floor, it feels like—"

"Good idea." I toe off my shoes and lean back against a pillow. The firelight reflects on her deep auburn hair, and the effect is mesmerizing. I must be staring because she gives me a timid smile, and her tongue flicks out over her bottom lip.

"Now, where were we?" she asks, leaning on her forearm, edging closer to me. She's so fucking sexy. I mirror her position on the floor, lying on my side.

I kiss her softly. A simple press of my lips against hers. An innocent kiss that says I'm interested. And I'm hopeful. I like her. And I want to get to know her. I find her intriguing. And charming.

Adrenaline courses through my veins. Our kisses deepen. Her body lines up along mine, then over mine. Her hands knit in my hair, and as with the switch on the wall, flames flick to life. Her warm skin blankets mine, and her thigh slides between my legs.

I groan at the pressure against my groin. Her hips rock above me, and the base of my spine tightens. It's glorious. She is glorious. I roll her onto her back, taking control.

"Too much?" she asks. The corners of her lips raise and form a sexy-as-fuck smile. I hold myself above her, on my forearms. Her hair sprawls out on the pillow. Her creamy pale skin flushes. As she spread her legs, welcoming me against her, the hem of her dress rises above her knee. I toy with the hem of the dress. She's wearing stockings. They're silky to the touch, and the pads of my fingers explore as our kiss heats. The stocking is smooth, and then I hit skin. Skin and a buckle, and I have to see. *Holy shit.* She's wearing creamy thigh highs and a garter belt.

Her hand grips my ass then shifts to the front. Those green eyes dare me as she cups my erection, and I close my eyes. *Fuck.*

"Do you like that?" Her teasing, forward tone snaps my willpower.

"Way too much." My mouth claims hers, only this time, there is nothing gentle about it. She tugs on my shirt as I explore beneath her dress, along the curve of her hips, her ass, her back.

Cool air envelops my torso as my shirt lands on the sofa. She raises her arms as I lift her dress high above her and send the garment sailing through the air after my shirt. Her fingers work my belt buckle as I unsnap her white bra.

I softly push her back onto a pillow, allowing myself a moment to take her in. *Hark the Angels.* She is divine laid out on my floor. Her dark hair spreads out all around with glints of red, her full, milky-white breasts, and light-colored nipples beg to be tasted, and her narrow waist tapers to a white garter over a sliver of silk with tiny candy canes across it.

She is every fantasy and then some. I yearn to taste every single inch. I want photos. I never want to forget the way she looks tonight.

"You're gorgeous," I tell her.

"I have a thing for lingerie." Her teeth sink into her lower lip. She's reticent, and that won't do.

"My new thing is you in lingerie." For all things holy, I speak the truth.

I begin my journey by claiming her lips once more, then trailing kisses from her ear, down her delicate neck, to her breasts. I suck in her nipple, savoring the way it pebbles from the feel of the moisture of my tongue. She hisses and mewls, and her hips shift beneath me as I bestow attention on each of her breasts, and stroke the curve of her waist, and then remove those cotton candy cane panties. I hold them up in my hand and ball them up.

"I'm keeping these. Thank you for my Christmas gift."

"You have a thing for panties?"

"No. I've never claimed a pair before. But I want these. I want to remember this." A nagging voice scolds, reminding me I wasn't going to do this again. That I would do things differently this time around. But that was before I knew she wore thigh highs.

She is a vision. A tasty treat. And I spend time showing her how much I treasure the Christmas gift before me. Her thighs clasp my ears as my fingers glide in and out of her wet, inviting channel while my tongue licks and I suck and nip. She fists one of the pillows. She moans and lets out a chorus of little sounds that have me teetering on the edge of an explosion of my own. With one last moan, she half-raises off the floor then collapses onto her back.

"Oh, my god. You didn't do that last time." I chuckle as I place kisses along her inner thighs, then along her smooth belly and over her breasts and nipples and her throat.

When I arrive back at her lips, she holds my jaw with both hands and says, "Thank you."

I kiss her hard. I love the feel of her below me, and I love that she seems to love her taste. We could end the night like this, kissing and cuddling, and it would be perfect. But her fingers slip around my painfully engorged erection, and any thought of that kind of conclusion goes up the chimney.

"Do you have a condom?" She pushes me onto my back, and I watch as she scrambles over me, her breasts jiggling, as she removes my trousers and boxers.

"Yes." Praise all the powers above. Yes, I have one. It's been years since I actually needed one on hand for random hook-ups. Those days were long gone. I dated now. And as I ripped the foil package and rolled the condom on, and gaze into green eyes I've never quite forgotten, it hits me. Those random hook-up days are not a part of my future.

I wondered about Nora for years. Thought of her with regrets. I should've treated her better. I at least owed her a call. I had promised. And yet, here she is, trusting me and giving me a second chance. This time around, I will not blow it.

Her legs wrap around me, and I pause only long enough for our gazes to lock as I thrust inside. She tilts her head back and fuck if she doesn't tighten around me.

"Breathe," I gasp.

She opens her eyes and sucks in a gulp of air. A smile dances across her lips. "Sorry, it's been a while. You're…big." *And you're fucking perfect.*

I pull out then slowly reenter, watching her carefully.

"This okay?"

"Yes, yes."

And then I lose myself in her kisses and in her body as we find our rhythm together. I barely register my throbbing knees against the hardwood. The entire room swirls into an oasis of blinking lights and complete elation. She reaches between us, and I almost explode as she toys with her clit. Her muscles coax my cock, pleasure surges in my lower spine, and I'm a mile high in the sky, taking a ride on the world's most magical sleigh. I pulse out my release with a loud roar.

IN THE MORNING, A VIBRATING NOISE EASES ME FROM A deep, full slumber. As consciousness rises, a warm, soft, naked body presses to mine. The sheet drapes the curve of her waist below her bare breasts. *Mouthwatering.* Every part of me wants to ignore the call of my phone and enjoy the delight in my bed, but instead of reaching for the sugar plum, with a groan, I pick up my phone. The text from the attending doctor notes that I don't have to come in. But this is my patient, and in the last ten days, I've operated on him twice.

I get dressed as quietly as possible. I pull out a notepad, and as the tip of my pen touches the paper, an inner voice whispers, *Wake her.* Leaving a note, even though it isn't at all the same thing as eight years ago, feels too much like a repeat.

So, I brush the tip of her nose with mine, then lightly press my lips to hers. I can't resist cupping her breast and flicking the nipple with my thumb. Her eyelids flutter open.

"Morning, sexy." Against the white of my sheets, her eyes are a lighter shade of green, and there's a bluish rim. Golden specks coat her irises. "I've got to run into the hospital."

She clutches the sheet and raises it over her breasts. I press my lips to her forehead.

"You can stay as long as you want. I don't know how long I'll be." If I have to open him back up again, I could be gone all day. "I'm leaving my extra key right here. You can use it to lock up if you do leave, okay?"

resent Day

Nora

THE HINT OF FRAGRANT PINE FILLS THE VACANT ROOM. Needles litter the floor in a circle beneath the tree and all over the thin red felt tree skirt. Instead of the sparkling tree from last night, a short tree with scraggly and uneven branches stands in the corner. It's a classic Charlie Brown tree.

The sparsely furnished apartment has a barely lived-in quality. The kitchen counters hold nothing, not even a bowl for keys. A copy of the *Journal of the American College of Cardiology* sits on the coffee table, and another journal with a similar name across the spine rests below it. A small silver remote and a lamp decorate the side table. A large, framed photograph of snowy mountains hangs on one wall. The snowy landscape has a professional quality. The solid black frame feels high-end and expensive.

I rub the key back and forth with my thumb. Did I make an enormous mistake last night? Repeat a mistake I swore I wouldn't repeat?

I pull on my coat and turn the doorknob. In doing so, I recognize the solid, sturdy knob. It will lock behind me. I find the paper and leave him a note.

ASHTON - YOUR DOOR WILL LOCK BEHIND ME. HERE'S your key. Thank you for a wonderful Christmas.
   -Nora

FRIGID AIR GREETS ME OUTSIDE, AND I CLUTCH MY coat as I hurry across the two blocks to my apartment. I only warm as I climb the last flight of stairs. I don't regret spending time with Ashton. I don't regret last night. I don't regret what we did, not exactly. But I hate the way I feel right now. There's this uncertainty that is all too familiar. Will he call? Or won't he? Will this be a repeat of so many years ago?

Yes, I could have taken his key. That would ensure I'd see him again. But if he calls again, I want it to be because he wants to call. Not because a hook-up has something of his to return. I don't want to be an obligation.

I shower in my apartment and get dressed. I check my phone. I make coffee. I read news articles, wasting time until I need to leave to volunteer. There's no need to check the phone because I've been reading from it. I plug it in the wall before leaving and purposefully leave it behind. I can't check it if it's not with me. It's this feeling right here that I hate. The uncertainty. If I had just left, if I hadn't pushed myself on him, I wouldn't be in this situation. I wouldn't be left wondering. These nerves in my belly are worse than the nerves before a date. Did he like me? That question might be the most painful in the world.

Back in the kitchen at Crossroads, I wrap a white apron around my waist and smile at several of the volunteers. The day after Christmas, there's always a surplus of volunteers. Every station has more than one person. Carlos approaches me and gestures to the dining area.

"I think you might be more needed outside," he says.

"What's going on?"

"Taylor's not looking too happy."

"Oh, no."

"Oh, yeah."

Outside in the dining room, light laughter and conversation fill the room. Today we are serving peanut butter and jelly sandwiches and bananas. It's the basic post-Christmas lunch. I recognize several of our regulars among those sitting in clusters along the long cafeteria-style tables. In the back of the room, sitting off by herself, Taylor stirs a paper cup. A tea string hangs over the side.

"Hey, how's it going?" I keep my tone cheery. The sad eyes that rise to greet me punch me in the gut.

"Hey."

"What's wrong?"

"Relapsed. I'm probably going to lose her." *Shit.* The light reflects heavily over her glassy eyes. I sink onto the bench across from her.

"What happened?"

"It was Christmas night. She'd gone back home. Not my home, the foster home. I felt so lonely. I was just going to have one drink. I thought that Christmas would be the one day of the year that I allowed myself a drink. Ray, my boyfriend, said one drink wouldn't hurt. But I didn't stop at one drink."

"Did you shoot up?" Her pupils appear normal. She's not quivering. I don't see sweat.

"No. I drank a lot. Ray had some cocaine. I don't think I did any. I'm not feeling like it today. But I blacked out. If they run a drug test and I fail it, there's no way the judge is going to give me custody." My mother had this problem. She got so close to getting me back, and then she'd fail a drug test. Or, at least, that's what the case records showed. As a child, I hadn't been made aware of all of the ups and downs. "One drink. That's all it was supposed to be."

"If you're an addict, you can't even have one drink. Have you ever had gene testing done?"

Taylor shakes her head as her fingers wrap around a paper coffee cup. They aren't trembling. Her skin color is normal, but there are shadows below her eyes. Those could be from lack of sleep and dehydration. She'd said she'd been addicted to meth, not alcohol. Maybe last night, she really did only drink alcohol. If so, she'd still pass a drug test.

"I've been tested," I tell her. "I have two of the genes, but not all of them. You might have all of them. I suspect my mother did. There are certain genes that make you more susceptible to addiction. But even though I don't have all the genes, it scares me. I don't like how I make bad decisions with alcohol." The last thing I want is to go down the addiction slide, like my mother and so many of the people who walked through the doors at Crossroads. Of course, I couldn't blame last night on alcohol.

"Not that that's stopped me from making bad decisions."

"You make bad decisions?" I can tell by the way Taylor rears back and cocks her head that she doesn't believe me.

"Believe it or not, there's not a single person alive who hasn't made a bad decision at some point. It's the human condition."

"I keep repeating my bad decisions."

"Yes. And no. You slipped, had one wild night, and instead of going on a binge, you're sitting here drinking tea and counting days again. That's a step forward. No one said the path out of rock bottom would be easy, but it's a day at a time, remember? You're gonna get there. Now you know—no drinks. At all."

"Three hundred and ninety-five days. That's how long I'd been sober."

"And you can do it again. At least this time, you didn't lose your job."

"If I have a positive drug test, I won't get that apartment. Ray, I know he had 'em. He says he didn't let me do nothing, but I don't know if he's lying."

"If you can't trust him, you shouldn't be with him."

"I know."

"Taylor, I hope you don't mind my saying so, but he doesn't have your best interest at heart. Anyone who encourages you to drink doesn't have your best interest at heart."

"I just get so lonely."

"I know. But you've got to stay focused. Your daughter needs you. She loves you."

"Ray, he likes to party."

"I understand. But your daughter? She's more important than any man."

"You're right."

"Eventually, you're going to get through this." I hold her hands and squeeze. For all I know, Taylor could be on a path similar to my mom, but it feels like she needs the positive energy and thoughts.

"You really believe that?"

"I do."

"And you did something bad?"

I hadn't really ever done anything bad. I'd always been too scared. Unless you counted sleeping with Ashton as bad. When I said I made mistakes, I was thinking of last night. I might regret it, but I don't count it as bad. A grown woman is entitled to have sex if she wants. But I always categorized my first night with Ashton as a poor decision, mainly because it hurt so much when he didn't call. And here I went and did it again. I should have taken things slower. I shouldn't have gotten so carried away. Taylor waits patiently for my answer.

"Well, I don't have a child." Her eyes tear up, and

guilt jabs me. I don't want to be cruel, but she needs to understand that there are levels to bad decisions. In my book, when you have a child, and your decision means your child becomes the custody of the state, well, it's the worst. But I don't need to say that to her. "But I tend to be less inhibited when I'm drinking. I've done things I regret. But more like hook-ups. Once I vomited in the back of a cab." Taylor doesn't so much as crack a smile.

"Your mom, she had my addiction, right? Meth?"

I nodded.

"Have you ever done it?"

"No." I probably wouldn't recognize it if I saw it, but I hated the substance. I hated the destruction it left in its wake.

"You're a good person." Taylor's dark brown eyes hold too much admiration for me.

"I don't know about that. I've just always been too scared I'd be like my mom. I can't imagine, no matter how much I had to drink, I'd ever try meth. I hate it too much. It took my mom away."

"Everyone has their struggles." Taylor pulls on the string, and the teabag circles through the hot, murky water. "Doesn't make them good or bad. I don't know your mom, but I'd bet she had her own struggles. Besides addiction. Or maybe you both were opposites. Maybe she let loose, and you're her opposite. I hope Reese is my opposite."

"When's your next meeting?"

"In an hour. That's why I'm hanging out here." They hold the meetings in the basement.

"Want company?"

"They wouldn't want that. But thank you for asking. Maybe for an open meeting?"

"Any time."

"And if you ever need help loosening up, let me know. I got advice to give."

"I'll keep that in mind. But I've been taking some risks." Thinking back to last night, yes, I'd put myself out there. *No, thanks. I'm good on the risks.*

"The greatest mistake in life is to be continually afraid you'll make one," Taylor mumbles into her tea.

"Where'd you hear that?"

"A meeting."

"Don't let the past steal your present." That's one of the quotes I'd heard ages ago, and I smile as I say it back to her.

"Our greatest glory consists not in not falling, but in rising up every time you fall. That one keeps me going."

"It's a good one. There's a quote from Ralph Waldo Emerson I've always liked. It kept me moving forward." She tilts her head, waiting for it. "The only person you are destined to become is the person you decide to be."

resent Day

NORA

IN ADVERTISING, A STRESSFUL SITUATION MEANS AN unhappy client. Maybe an ad didn't do well. Or someone else's creative got picked for a campaign. In Ashton's job, people live or die. He has to tell people if their loved one survived surgery. And this patient had weighed on him. He didn't say much about him, but the weight hung in his expression as he shared his frustration that the man hadn't followed his at-home instructions.

I shouldn't have left that key behind. There isn't a voice whispering in my ear as much as a nagging inner jab. And what will he think when he gets home and sees it? If the roles had been reversed, and it was me coming home, seeing that note and key would crush me.

I'd watched *Grey's Anatomy* and *Scrubs* enough to know that coffee machines are omnipresent in a hospital. But everyone likes Starbucks, right? He might not want it, but the gesture, well, doing something thoughtful for someone else is never a waste.

As I waited in line at Starbucks, not one but three couples wait in line in front of me. I'd always told myself I was better off being single. That I was happy being single. Never allowing myself to depend on someone else. But the lonely trajectory I have placed myself on doesn't have a bright outlook. Sure, I stayed clear of drugs, and I now have a sizeable 401K and my own apartment without a roommate, but I have remained on the fringe of friend groups. In eight years, I haven't changed jobs. Admittedly, Evolve treats me well, and Anna always looks out for me, and the place has become my family. But recruiters had called, and I'd refused to even talk to them. Who knew what other options I had turned my back on? I even turned down advancements within my agency, all to stay under the same boss, afraid that our friendship wouldn't survive a job change.

The receptionist at the main desk in Sloan Memorial blinks multiple times when I ask to see Dr. Daughtridge. As the older woman searches through a directory on the monitor that I imagine holds hundreds of names, the ridiculousness of stopping by unannounced at a mammoth New York hospital sets in. He's a surgeon. He could be in surgery.

"He's not answering his office line. Is he expecting you?" Her eyes narrow. "Are you a patient?"

"No. It's okay. Thank you." I hustle out of the lobby before the woman can reprimand me. Of course, people don't just stop by to see surgeons. Yes, people don't normally stop by friend's apartments in New York, and he did that, but this hospital must have thousands of employees. And surgeons probably need to remain washed and disinfected. That means welcoming random street people up to the surgery ward or wing or whatever you call it would be a no-no. I should have just texted. *And maybe if you'd been carrying your phone around with you, like a normal person, you would've thought of that.* I dump the second coffee into a trash can on the corner and speed up the avenue.

As I round the corner to my street, I falter.

Ashton sits on the bench in front of my building in jeans, a jacket, and running shoes. His head is bent down, focused on the phone in his hand.

"Hey, there. What're you doing here?" Hearing me, he raises his head and grins.

"Well, I got back to my place and found the key. I texted you, and you didn't return my text."

"I don't have my phone. I volunteered again."

"I hoped that was it. Anyway, I should have the rest of the day off. Another colleague is officially on call. Wanted to see if you'd be interested in spending the rest of the day together? You still have off, right?"

The man practically chased me down. He likes me.

He rises from the bench and shoves his hands into his pockets. His shoulders round, and he rocks back on his heels. The moment is surreal.

"I don't mean to pressure you. But I have all those leftovers. I still have a tree with lights. Figured we could watch movies or just hang out. Maybe go for a walk in the park later? I've been meaning to catch one of those horse-drawn carriages one of these days. We can do whatever you want." He runs his fingers through his hair, roughing it up. "Look, in some ways, I am the same guy from eight years ago. I have a demanding schedule. I can't change that. But one thing I can change is your fear that I won't call or that I'll disappear. I've never given a woman a key before, but I did that for you this morning because I need you to know I'm also a different guy. Before, at that stage in my life, I couldn't handle a relationship. I think I can now. Or at least I'd like to try. You're a good friend of my sister's—a friend more than a colleague. I promise you, if things aren't working out, I'll talk to you. I won't just disappear. And I'd really like to see you again."

"I stopped by the hospital. With a coffee for you."

"You did? Is that it?" He gestures to the coffee in my hand.

"No. I threw it away. The front desk couldn't reach you, and I realized it probably wasn't a good idea to stop by unannounced—"

"I don't think anyone's ever stopped by to see me at work. Well, Anna, but I met her in front of the ER. Does stopping by the hospital mean we're good?"

"Yes. We're good. It was never so much a matter of forgiving you as trusting you. But I want to try. After all, I believe in second chances."

HAVE YOURSELF A MERRY LITTLE CHRISTMAS

ne Year Later

ASHTON

THE SIDEWALKS ARE FILLED WITH A MIXTURE OF residents and tourists. I am late, and I jog down the concrete around the slower pedestrians. A woman's giant shopping bag knocks my knee, and it hits the ground with a thud.

"Sorry. I'm sorry." I expect a glare, but she's chatting with her friend and barely gives me a second glance. I continue, weaving in and out on the sidewalk, like a race car driver in a career-making Indy 500.

When I finally arrive at our apartment, I shove open the door, bend to untie my running shoes, and call out, "Sorry I'm late. I got pulled into a discussion about a surgery tomorrow." I have ten minutes to shower and put on a tux. *Doable. Should I delay the driver?*

Nora enters the room, and I pause, one shoe still halfway on. She's wearing a form-fitting, forest green full-length dress. The V-neck slopes teasingly low. Her auburn hair bounces in loose, full curls around her shoulders.

"Wow." She steals my breath. "You look gorgeous."

"Anna, Delilah, Olivia, and I went and had our hair, nails, and makeup done. I was nervous about the makeup because you know they always put on a little too much, but what do you think?"

Nora approaches, angling her face up to me for closer inspection. My fingers roam the smooth, cool silk of the gown over her hips, and I kiss my beautiful girlfriend. It turns out, even with an intensive work schedule, with a little effort, for the right woman, I can nail the dating game. She ended up spending so much time at my place that I eventually convinced her to take the next step. She moved in Thanksgiving week, and I had the best Thanksgiving of my adult life.

My delectable, gorgeous girlfriend tastes like

peppermint, and her curves press against me in all the right places. My scrubs do nothing to hide my attraction to her, and I back her up against the wall. As I skim those smooth curves, the absence of one thing becomes paramount.

"No panties?"

Her pale skin flushes and the tips of her fingers trail her now swollen lips. "You'll have to wait and see. Now, go get ready."

"How badly do you want to go tonight?" Because I don't want to leave our apartment at all. Watching her all night, knowing she might wear nothing at all underneath that sexy-as-fuck dress, will be torture. Exquisite torture, yes, but I'll be on edge the entire evening.

"Go get your shower. I'll be right here. Reapplying my lipstick."

My thumb flicks her perky, erect nipple through the silk, and then I force myself to the shower.

This year, our apartment feels like home. From the day after Thanksgiving, Nora began decorating. We'd spent each weekend shopping around town and online for holiday decorations. The Sunday after Thanksgiving, we'd purchased a full-size eight-foot tree and paid for delivery. Nora declared we found the perfect tree because she liked the way it smelled. The living room had all the decorations, but it wasn't the decorations that made it feel like home for me. The tinsel didn't make it Christmas. Love made it Christmas.

I've never been so in love with anyone in all my life. As I pass under the archway into our bedroom, I notice the mistletoe ball hanging, and I reach up and tap it with my finger. The green ball with red berries twirls on its hook.

I could orchestrate my plan right here in our first apartment. But, of course, Delilah will kill me if I don't show. She and Anna went all in to help me create an unforgettable moment.

As I shower, I second-guess our plans. I've shared most of my concerns with Anna, mostly via text, since these days, when I see her, Nora is always with us.

. . .

MY SISTER'S WORD IS GOOD. I KNOW THIS. BUT STILL. Nora will be swarmed by strangers afterward. Nerves flare in my gut. I peer down the hallway to ensure she isn't close by and slide open the small top drawer in our dresser. The velvet ring box is light in my hand, and I snap the lid open, double-checking the ring remains inside. With a solid snap, the box closes, and I drop it into my trouser pocket. In the mirror, the bulge on the side of my leg is too noticeable. I pull back my coat and slip it into an interior pocket closer to my waist, just as the love of my life enters the room.

"You are the gorgeous one. Yum." She sets about tying my bow tie. She hasn't always known how to do that. But this isn't our first dressy event. She studied how to do it on YouTube last spring for one of the hospital charity events.

She angles her face upward to lightly press her glossy lips to mine. My hands possessively fall on the curves of her bottom. *Mine*.

"You're taller," I observe.

"Anna talked me into some sexy high heels."

"Well, this year, hopefully, you won't feel the need to run across cobblestones to get away from me."

Her eyes shine a light green with flecks of gold. I love how her irises serve as mood barometers. If she were sad, they shaded bluer. If they were dark green, I'd really pissed her off. And now, with the gold interlaced, she is happy. And so am I.

I follow her out of our bedroom, stopping her for one delicious kiss beneath the mistletoe. I could do it right here, beneath the mistletoe, or in front of our first tree. But the Empire State Building, and my sister, beckon.

I fidget in the back seat as the reality of what I have planned sets in. Nora gazes out the window, taking in the holiday lights with the delight of a child. Our hands are locked.

My confidence she'll say yes is pretty strong. We've talked about it more than once. She told me she wants children–more than one, she'd said. If something happened to her, she didn't want her children out there in the world alone. And, given how much I love my sister, I agree.

"So, two?" I'd asked. We'd been lying in bed, and her head rested on my chest as my fingers tangled with her strands.

"Yes. Three in the city would be difficult, don't you think? You can't fit three car seats in a back row, and it's just...life is designed for a family of four."

"Seems logical. So, you're okay with the idea of remaining in the city?" I needed to remain close to the hospital.

"In this scenario, are you my husband?" She dropped a kiss over my sternum, and I'd swear warmth penetrated the organ beneath.

"Yes. Obviously." My answer earned me another round of lovemaking that night. She'd been mine then, and I had known even before then, I wanted her forever.

· · ·

THE CAR PULLS UP TO THE FRONT OF THE EMPIRE State Building. The friends rented out the State Grill and Bar. And Sam and Olivia have arranged for all guests to be able to access the top, from dessert time on through the end of the night. Jackson hinted it cost a small fortune, and I can't help but wonder if maybe they changed venues this year explicitly to give me this storybook moment. I cringe at the thought. My brother-in-law might be financially successful to a degree a surgeon in the city will never match, but I don't like leveraging him or his connections.

Jackson and Anna stand on the sidewalk, both bundled up in black dress coats and gloves. As the car pulls to a halt, Jackson steps up and opens the back door for Nora.

As I exit the vehicle, sliding out on the bench seat, Anna wraps Nora up in a hug.

"Are you two greeting everyone outside?" Nora asks. I understand her dismay, as greeting hundreds of guests on a cold winter night wouldn't be desirable at all.

"Only special ones. We've arranged for some private excursions to the top. After dinner, it will surely be a crowd." She hands a golden plastic piece to Nora, and she smiles over her shoulder at me. "You two need to go on up now. There will be a person behind a small bar at the top, and you can have your cocktails up on the platform. Have fun." I roll my eyes as my sister lets out an indiscreet squeal.

Jackson pounds my back, and there's a gruff, barely audible, "Good luck."

Well, if she wasn't suspicious something might be happening tonight, now she is. Thanks, guys.

My ears pop as the powerful elevator climbs a hundred and two floors. We both still wear our dress coats. I remain confident in her answer, yet my fingers tremble slightly. Enough I couldn't do surgery if I wanted at this moment. I recite my speech in my head, knowing the moment has come. In some ways, we've already committed to each other. I settled any lingering uncertainties she might have harbored almost a year ago, mostly by remaining in contact and showing up.

The elevator doors open. I've been here before, but the room had been filled with tourists. Now, we are the only occupants. We step out onto the platform, and true to Anna's word, an attendant stands behind a temporary bar, bundled up and prepared to offer us champagne.

I guide Nora past the man with a brief nod. I hope we'll be coming back to him for a private celebration glass momentarily.

Nora gasps as she steps onto the viewing platform. The city stretches out before us, a mass of twinkling lights extending as far as the ocean. Taller buildings light the landscape to the south.

"Wow. It's spectacular. Gorgeous. It's nice that they're giving people some private time up here, don't you think? It'll make the night memorable for sure." She steps away, prepared to check out the view from all sides. But my heart races, and it's impossible to wait.

I locate the ring box in my jacket and drop to one knee, and Nora's gloved hands cover her mouth.

"Nora, a year ago, you gave me a second chance. And I'll forever be grateful you did because, over the last year, I've gotten to know you. Really know you. You've become my best friend. The one who pulls me away from work. The one who gives me something to look forward to coming home to. When I look to the future, I can't imagine it without you. Nora, will you marry me? Will you be mine for life?"

"Oh, my god, yes. Yes."

I fumble with the closed ring box and lift the ring. Anna helped me pick it out. Her bottom lip quivers as I slide it on her finger.

I stand and wipe a tear from her cheek. And everything blurs as my emotions build. I crush her to me and spin her around. And then we kiss. I pour my heart into our kiss as love and contentment and happiness and relief burst within me.

We stand there, holding each other, grinning. Only then do I glance up and realize I messed it all up.

"I was supposed to ask you over there." I point.

"Why?"

"See the mistletoe? Anna and Delilah picked the location. We're supposed to be over there. I guess it's the best view."

"No." Her firm answer broaches no room for discussion.

"No?"

"The best view is right here. I don't need mistletoe. I don't need a spectacular view. You. You're all I need. You could have asked me in our apartment, and I'd never forget the moment."

"And that's one of the many, many reasons I love you."

The Westside Series

When the Stars Align (Jackson and Anna)

Trust Me (Sam and Olivia)

Walk the Dog (Mason and Delilah)

Lost on the Way (Jason and Maggie)

Chasing Frost (Chase and Sadie)

Haven Island Series

Rogue Wave (Tate and Luna)

Adrift (Gabe and Poppy)

First Light (Cali & Logan)

Twisted Vines Series - Coming 2022!

Crushed (Erik and Vivi)

Loved (David and Kairi)

Screwed (Trevor and Stella)

ACKNOWLEDGMENTS

Notes & Acknowledgment

I hope you enjoyed reading *Misplaced Mistletoe*! I hadn't planned on doing Ashton's (er...Bobby's) story. But a reader wrote and asked. And I have to admit, that was pretty exciting.

Novellas are not my thing. I don't usually read them, and I've never written one before. But I had a one-month gap in my writing calendar, and I had an idea for a holiday novella...and now you have *Misplaced Mistletoe*.

Originally, I wrote it in the third person. (What a mistake). Then I converted to the first person. A huge thanks goes out to Casey from Heart Full of Ink. I'd been ready to throw in the towel and press delete, and she gave me some helpful pointers, and I realized I'd lost some important aspects in my third to first conversion. Then Lori Whitwam, the keeper of all the words, helped me further refine it.

Two author friends beta read for me (pre-editing!) and helped to further improve the rhythm of the holiday jingle. Dianne May and Carly Autumn…thank you!

Last but most definitely not least, I'd like to thank my ARC readers. You guys rock, and I so much appreciate your volunteering to be on the team and then going out and sharing your reviews. You make all the difference when it releases out in the world.

Most of all, dear readers—THANK YOU! Thank you for picking up this book and giving it a chance. I love to hear from readers. You can contact me through my website at www.isabeljoliebooks.com and also sign up to find out when my next book will be available. Thanks again and again for your support!

One of the things I love most about holiday movies is the softly falling snow. Have you ever noticed it almost always snows in movies, even in New York City, where it almost never snows before Christmas? I purposefully didn't include snowflakes in this novella (or at least the real kind) because you know what? You can have Christmas magic no matter the weather. My holiday wish for you is that you have your own merry little Christmas with those you love, no matter where you live, with or without mistletoe!

ABOUT THE AUTHOR

Isabel Jolie, aka Izzy, lives on a lake, loves dogs of all stripes, and if she's not working, she can be found reading, often with a glass of wine in hand. In prior lives, Izzie worked in marketing and advertising, in a variety of industries, such as financial services, entertainment, and technology. In this life, she loves daydreaming and writing contemporary romances with real, flawed characters and inner strength.

Sign-up for Izzy's newsletter to keep up-to-date on new releases, promotions and giveaways. Or stalk her on your favorite platform. And no, she's not on TikTok. Her teen keeps telling her to stay away…
https://isabeljoliebooks.com/#newsletter